Everyone's a Critic

DRAMA!

The Four Dorothys

Everyone's a Critic

Don't miss the next show!

Show, Don't Tell

DRAMA!

Everyone's a Critic

Paul Ruditis

Simon Pulse
NEW YORK   LONDON   TORONTO   SYDNEY

This book is a work of fiction. Any references to historical events, real people, or real locales are used fictitiously. Other names, characters, places, and incidents are the product of the author's imagination, and any resemblance to actual events or locales or persons, living or dead, is entirely coincidental.

SIMON PULSE

An imprint of Simon & Schuster Children's Publishing Division
1230 Avenue of the Americas, New York, NY 10020
Copyright © 2007 by Paul Ruditis
All rights reserved, including the right of reproduction in whole
or in part in any form.
SIMON PULSE and colophon are registered trademarks
of Simon & Schuster, Inc.
Designed by Mike Rosamilia
The text of this book was set in Weiss.
Manufactured in the United States of America
First Simon Pulse edition October 2007
2 4 6 8 10 9 7 5 3 1
Library of Congress Control Number 2007925256
ISBN-13: 978-1-4169-3392-2
ISBN-10: 1-4169-3392-1

☆ For Babe, Amy, and Brané ☆

The Odd Couple

"SOMETIMES, I JUST WANT TO RIP YOUR HEAD OFF, DISEMBOWEL YOU, AND FEED YOU TO THE SHARKS!"

There's a pretty picture.

That dainty line of dialogue was courtesy of Hope Rivera, one of my best friends and banter partners. Hope was in the process of breaking up with her boyfriend and my *ex*-best friend, Drew. Not that this was anything new to them. At last count, Hope and Drew had broken up at least a dozen times. It's just that there was a note of finality in this particular fight. A note that was both sweet and sour at the same time, much like the chicken I was dining on with Suze Finberg as we shared a blanket while trying not to listen. Or, more specifically, trying not to look like we were listening, while we listened. Just like everyone else on our section of beach. Not that any of us could have missed it. Hope's voice does kind of carry.

"DON'T YOU DARE BLAME ME! YOU KNOW I DON'T HAVE A PROBLEM WITH IT. THAT'S ALL YOU."

We hadn't quite figured out what they were fighting over, but apparently it was Drew's issue, not Hope's. At least, if her latest outburst was to be believed.

"ALL YOU, BABY!"

Then again, it wasn't like she was having one of her more rational moments.

"How's the chicken, Bryan?" Suze asked me from our little patch of sand as we took in the unexpected dinner theater.

"Tastes like alligator," I said. "And the quiche?"

"Real men would totally eat it."

"Good to know," I said. The party could use a real man or two as far as I was concerned.

Speaking of not-so-real men, we were sitting on the sand outside of Eric Whitman's Mondo Malibu Dream House for the Start-of-Summer Beach Party. Our host, Eric, was nowhere to be found while his best friend's relationship was going through the wringer. *Nice.* Meanwhile, I was trying to avoid my wondering wanderings since Eric wasn't the only one missing at the moment.

A cute waiter circulated by our blanket, and Suze and I grabbed some vegetable pot stickers and continued to watch the show.

"I DON'T CARE IF EVERYONE CAN HEAR ME!"

That much was apparent.

Hope and Drew had been dating on and off for about . . . well, it seemed like forever, but it had been around three years.

I'd love to be able to tell some meet cute story about the first time they ever saw each other, but that would have happened back when Drew and I met her in kindergarten. The only thing cute about that meet was that I was positively adorable in my first-day-of-school outfit: GapKids from head to toe. Now that I think of it, I looked a bit like ye olde tyme newsboy, complete with strategically distressed messenger bag.

As for how the dating thing started, I'm not really sure. The two of them had never seemed particularly close while we were growing up. Then, one day after Drew and I stopped being best friends, I heard he was going out with Hope. That was later confirmed when I saw them holding hands between classes. Sorry, it's not a more exciting story, but since I wasn't in it all that much, how exciting could it have been?

"[CENSORED]!" (The language Hope was using, however, had gotten *very* exciting. Too exciting for me to even write here. Use your imagination.)

Just so you don't go thinking I'm ignoring Drew's part of the fight by only including Hope's dialogue, you'd be wrong. Drew wasn't saying much during the encounter. And what he had said had been spoken so softly that it was almost impossible to hear. Trust me, Suze and I tried. It wasn't easy. We had only managed to piece together the phrase "I'm putting you under a hex." And that couldn't be right. Aside from the fact that Drew didn't really go in for the occult, Hope was fairly religious and took these things seriously. If he ever tried to put her under a hex, she probably would have hauled off and knocked him out. Nope. They had to be fighting about a more worldly subject matter.

If only we could come up with a word that rhymed with hex.

Of course, our attention was split at the moment. "Try the crab puffs," Suze said as she handed me one.

"You can't eat crab puffs." I needlessly reminded her of her food allergy.

"I know," she said. "That's why I want you to try one. So you can tell me what I'm missing."

I smiled as I popped a puff in my mouth and gave her a thumbs-up. It was a pretty good puff. It was also a pretty good time. I mean, for the two of us. Hope and Drew didn't seem to be having much fun.

"So . . . ," Suze said, drawing out the word like she was trying to figure out how to approach a subject.

"So . . . ," I replied, wondering where she was going with this. Suze wasn't usually one for vague opening statements.

"I've had a lot of fun hanging out since the prom," she said.

"Oh," I replied, knowing *exactly* where this was going.

Seeing how my other best friend, Sam, is now coupled with Eric, and Hope and Drew are—or *were*—also a couple, we'd been spending a lot of time hanging out as a group lately. Never big on being the fifth wheel, I'd been inviting Suze along whenever we went out, which wound up being every single weekend since the prom.

Now, let me be clear about this: I *never* asked Suze on a date. I *never*, in any way, implied that I liked her as more than a friend. I wouldn't do that to her. I wouldn't do that to anyone. It's one thing to not mention the fact that I'm gay to my friends. It's another thing entirely to live a lie and use some-one else in the process. I can't help it if she jumped to the wrong conclusion.

Can I?

"ARE YOU DONE?" Drew yelled at a volume that finally matched Hope's dulcet tones.

Whoa. Alert the media. Drew Campbell actually raised his voice.

Heads all over the beach turned in their direction, giving up any pretense of subtle eavesdropping, and stared, open-mouthed, at him. Outbursts like that were out of character for Drew. For Hope, it was second nature. But Drew? It was so shocking that Suze totally ignored me to watch what was happening. I'd have to thank Drew later for that.

"NO. I'M NOT DONE!" Hope yelled back.

"WELL, I AM!" Drew turned and stormed away from her . . . heading directly toward Suze and me.

My body went rigid. Why was he walking toward us? We didn't need to be in the middle of this. More specifically, *I* didn't need to be in the middle of this. I could see Hope readying her death glare. Whatever happened in the next few seconds could determine the entire course of my friendship with her. If she thought for a moment that I was on his side or rendering any kind of comfort, then she'd never speak to me again.

Okay, maybe I'm being a little melodramatic here, but you've never been under Hope's death glare, so don't judge.

Drew was getting closer. My mind was racing with things to say. Ways to make it clear that whatever they were fight-ing about, I was in Hope's corner. But, as Drew's face came closer, I could see the hurt in his eyes. It was the same expression he had when he learned the truth about the Easter Bunny. Most kids have a thing about Santa Claus, but Drew had always been into the bunny. Seriously. A cute little animal that brings you free candy? What's not to love? And on that day so many years ago, he rode his bike right to my place in search of solace and friendship.

Why in the world would he come to me for that now?

Drew stopped at the edge of our blanket, looking down at Suze and me. At least, I assume he was looking down at us. I was positively enthralled by the plate resting in my lap. The food we still hadn't tasted appeared to be absolutely delicious. So delicious, I felt it warranted my total and absolute attention.

I guess Suze had a problem with the awkward silence, because she was the first to speak. "Are you guys okay?" she asked.

I think Drew may have shrugged. I'm not sure as I was examining a particularly interesting pair of pigs-in-a-blanket at the time. Or would that be pig-in-a-blankets? Pigs-in-blankets?

"I'm going for a walk," Drew said. I watched his feet move away from us.

I kind of felt like he wanted someone to go with him. Like me, maybe. But I'm sorry . . . just because we'd been hanging out—in a group—a bit more over the past few weeks didn't mean we were buddy-buddy again. He ditched me as a friend years ago. Old wounds don't heal that easily. Providing solace and comfort to Drew was Eric's job now, not mine.

"Do they always fight like that?" Suze whispered once Drew was out of earshot. Hope was standing at the water's edge watching the sunset over the beach in her black one-piece bathing suit and matching black sarong. She had a bright blue flower in her hair. This part of Malibu was south-facing so the sun set over the beach to the right of us instead of over the water. She struck quite an imposing figure with the orange light on her tan skin.

I considered Suze's question. "Do they always fight? Yes. Like this? Not so much."

"Should someone say something?" she asked.

"I guess," I said, knowing that the *someone* she was referring to was probably me. But, to be honest, I didn't have a clue what the *something* would be to say. Getting in between Hope and anyone she was angry with was not something one did casually. Quite frankly, I didn't think it was any of my business. That, and I'm notoriously afraid of confrontation. And conflict. Now that I think of it, I don't like most words that begin with *con*. Except *conquistador*. That's just fun to say.

Conquistador.

"What did I miss?" Sam asked as she came out of Eric's house with her boyfriend following like an itty-bitty puppy dog. Like the kind some girls usually carry around in their purse. That poops on their car keys.

Sam and I had only been friends for a couple years, but she's totally the reason I believe in reincarnation. I don't usually go for that metaphysical stuff, but our bond was so strong from the first hello that we must have been friends in previous lives. Like she was Cleopatra and I was her purely platonic consort who would hang with her as the slave boys fed us grapes and fanned us with palm fronds.

Back in the present, I couldn't help but notice that Sam and Eric had been gone for an awfully long time. Maybe they were conjuring up some hexes. I surreptitiously checked to confirm that Sam was still wearing her silver unicorn necklace. (She once confided in me that she would only take that necklace off after she—how do I put this delicately—lost her virginal status.) I was relieved to see that it was comfortably in place at the base of her neck. Not that I understood why I was relieved. It's not like I'm secretly pining for my best friend. And don't go thinking I'm all in denial about my true feelings or anything. I'm really not interested in the girl. Or any girl for that matter.

And I'm certainly not interested in Eric.

"The end of the affair," I said. "It looks like true love has run its course for Hope and Drew."

"Again?" Sam asked.

"Again and for good, if you ask me," I said. "For really good."

The sun continued to set, taking on deeper shades of red as it dipped behind the houses to the west of us. Hope was actually quite beautiful standing there in profile as the shadows descended around her. I couldn't help myself. I grabbed my camera and took of picture of her in her melancholy.

"Bryan!" Sam smacked me on the shoulder.

"Can I help it if misery makes for a beautiful shot?"

"I better go see if she's all right," Sam said to Eric.

"I'll go check on Drew," Eric replied.

As the two of them walked in different directions, I called out, "I'll stay right here and finish dinner."

"Do you always make jokes in times of stress?" Suze asked once we found ourselves alone in the crowd again.

"I make jokes all the time," I said. "It's easier than dealing with reality."

Suze thought about what I was saying. "And exactly how much reality do you deal with around here?" She waved out toward the beach with the typically indescribable sunset. I guess she was right. Between us and the sunset were a bunch of beautiful Malibu teens frolicking in the sand. They weren't *all* model gorgeous, but they were all acting like they were. Like they were just waiting for paparazzi to show up. Then again, it is possible that some of them were actually expecting cameramen to swing by. They are the children of the glitterati, after all.

"Point taken," I said.

Suze cupped her hand over her eyes and looked directly into the fading light. "Twenty-four hours from now I'll be watching the sunset reflected off the top of the Chrysler Building."

"It's a hard-knock life," I said.

Suze's vacation was set to start the next day. Not that it was going to be much of a "vacation" since she was jetting off for an internship at Ellis Designs. That's the company owned by famous fashion designer Natalie Ellis, aka Hope's mom. This meant she was going to miss out on summer school with the rest of us.

Not that it was *really* summer school.

Now that our junior year at Orion Academy was over and we were all technically seniors, you'd think we'd get to kick back and relax without having to see the inside of our beloved school for another couple months. Wrong! First we had to get through the Orion Academy Summer Theatrical Program before the relaxing began. A two-week, intensive theater-training course that culminates in a full-scale, no-budget production. *Then*, it would be off on holiday.

Hope would join her mom in New York City. Sam's boyfriend, Eric, would visit his mom and her girlfriend in the Hamptons. At some point my mom and I would meet up with my father and summer on the coast for a week or two. I wasn't quite sure what coast we'd be summering on since my father bounces around the globe for his mysteriously boring job, but we'd have a good time.

Until then, with Suze gone, I'd be back to fifth-wheel status. That is, if both my best friends were still engaged in coupledom. As things currently stood, it didn't look all that likely.

I picked up my camera and started snapping shots of the fading light playing off the ocean. Sam and Hope stood off to the left of me, while Drew and Eric were off to my right. Leaving me stuck—physically and metaphorically—in the middle.

On a Clear Day
You Can See Forever

In the summer, it should be illegal for morning to begin before noon. Especially in Malibu. You'd think that living in one of the most famous beach communities in the world, it might be worthwhile to get up early and enjoy the day. Honestly? Unless you're a surfer, there's really no need.

Summer usually begins in the midst of June Gloom. That's when every morning starts off with a low marine layer, encasing the Malibu Colony in fog and cloud cover until much later in the day. And don't let the name fool you. June Gloom happens anytime in the year that it wants to. It's just worst when the beach-going is supposed to be the best. Not that it would make any difference in my case. Even if every day was bright and sunny, I'd still be as pale as the walking dead.

The other thing that should be illegal is going to school in the summer. Even though the Orion Academy Summer Theatrical Program isn't really like normal school, it still takes place *at* school. So, just when you thought you'd escaped, they pull you back in.

I was the first one in the parking lot. I blame my mom for that one. She agreed to watch one of her clients' Labradoodles. (That's a dog, if you don't know. A cross between a Labrador and a poodle.) Mom owns a doggie boutique on Melrose Avenue called Kaye 9. It caters to the pampered pooches of the pampered Hollywood elite . . . and anyone else who can afford to plunk down a hundred dollars for a dog's T-shirt.

I can't blame my mom entirely, though. You see, Canoodle— that's her name . . . Canoodle the Labradoodle—belongs to the headmaster of my school, Headmaster Collins. Mom had agreed to watch Canoodle while the headmaster and his wife were on a month-long tour of Europe. I doubt Mrs. Collins would have left her baby with us if she knew that Mom never let poor Canoodle past the kitchen and into the rest of the pristine house. We do have a big backyard for her to play in . . . Canoodle, I mean, not Mrs. Collins.

Typically, I'm big on dogs, but this particular Labra gets up at the crack of gloomy dawn to doodle and likes to wake up the entire house in the process. Then again, if I couldn't go to the bathroom unless someone opened a door for me, I guess I wouldn't be all that quiet in the morning either.

Here's the problem with starting your day early at Orion: If you get to school before the teachers, you can't get in. I hadn't known that before, never having started my day before the teachers. I guess that seems pretty obvious, but who can be logical at eight o'clock in the morning during the summer?

All I could do was sit in my car, Electra, staring out the window, wishing she had an iPod connection . . . or a CD player . . . or FM radio. That's the problem with driving a 1957 Ford Fairlane Skyliner that previously belonged to my grandfather: What I get in style I lose out in modern conveniences.

Another car finally pulled into the lot around eight thirty. I silently thanked the driver for saving me from staring at Electra's ceiling any longer. I immediately took back that appreciation when I saw who was behind the wheel.

Did I mention that the Orion Academy Soccer Program runs simultaneously alongside the Theater Program? Well, it does. And wouldn't you know, the first two members of the soccer team to show up would be Eric and Drew.

"This day's not getting any better," I mumbled as they parked right next to me. The *entire* parking lot was empty and they needed to park right beside Electra? I pulled the tip of my fedora down over my eyes and pretended to take a nap. I guess my performance wasn't all that convincing, because I soon heard a tap-tap-tapping at my window.

I peeked out from under the rim of my fedora. "Nobody's home."

Eric ignored my sarcasm. "Hey, Bryan. What are you doing here so early?" His voice was *way* too cheery for eight thirty in the morning. Ever since he and Sam started dating, he kept trying to be my friend. It was *really* annoying. Especially since, if I wasn't nice in return, I'd be the one coming off like an ass. Which, I guess I was being, but whatever.

"Trying to sleep," I replied.

"Why don't you do that at home?" Eric asked with actual concern in his voice. "Is everything okay? Suze's leaving for New York this morning, right?"

"I'm up," I said, lifting my fedora. The last thing I wanted was for this to become a *moment*.

I hopped out of Electra. Now that the rim of my fedora was out of my way and I had access to my full field of vision, I could see that Drew was a mess. Don't get me wrong. He was nicely outfitted in Hollister from head to toe, but he clearly hadn't slept at all since the Start-of-Summer Beach Party the night before.

"Is Sam here yet?" Eric asked me.

I made an exaggerated point of looking out over the empty parking lot. "Um . . . no."

"Did you guys hang out last night after the party?" Eric asked. "After you left with Hope."

I guess I was more awake than I thought, because I was on top of things enough to realize that Eric was trying to pump me for information about Hope for Drew. That was nice. Naive, but nice.

"Nope," I said. "Hope wanted to be alone."

"Oh," Eric said. He wasn't about to give up so easily. "Did you—"

"What are you wearing?" Drew interrupted.

He speaks.

"A shirt," I said. Actually, I was wearing an entire outfit: fedora, jeans, shoes, socks, underwear, and a shirt. But his eyes were focused on the shirt when he asked his question. I could understand why. It's really a great shirt. At first it seems like nothing more than a white T-shirt with this crazy black design covering the entire front and back. But after you stare at it for a while you realize that the design is actually a huge pile of skulls. Hundreds of these tiny skulls. Then, once you've seen the skulls, you can't help but see them every time you look at the shirt. Drew's the only person who's noticed so far.

Heck, I'd already worn the shirt twice before I first noticed it.

"It's . . . weird."

"Thanks," I said. Eric looked at the two of us like we were crazy. Like it was our fault that he wasn't observant.

Fortunately, people started filling the parking lot so we weren't stuck for awkward conversation much longer. Unfortunately, the people were mostly soccer players to whom I had nothing to say, so there was still some awkward standing around for a few minutes until Sam's mom pulled up to drop her daughter off. I hurried over to their car.

"Good morning, Anne," I said to Sam's mom, leaning in the passenger's side window.

"I didn't expect you to be here already," Anne replied. "This wouldn't have anything to do with Canoodle, would it?"

I blinked in shock. Anne was scary psychic on that one.

"Headmaster Collins is always complaining about having to walk Canoodle before the sun's up," she explained. Anne teaches English at Orion, so she knows a lot more about our headmaster than we do. "I guess he left that part out when he got your mom to watch her."

"Must've slipped his mind," I said, not even remotely giving our beloved headmaster the benefit of the doubt.

"I can't get out," Sam said to me.

"And you're telling me this, why?".

"Because you're hanging in my window," she said, giving the door a gentle shove into my torso.

"Allow me," I said, swinging the door open for her.

"Good morning," Eric said, with his hand out to help her out of the car as soon as I cleared the way. Had to give the guy points for being smooth. Don't worry, I was sure I could take those points away for some reason soon enough.

"I've got to get to school myself," Anne said. She was taking summer classes too, going for her master's. "Bryan, you're okay with taking Sam home?"

"No problem," I replied. And it wasn't, really. Sam lives in Santa Monica, which is only a short drive down the Pacific Coast Highway. The drive gets a little longer during the summer with all the beach traffic, but it's not that bad. Besides, the view is pretty nice along the way. Most of the surfers tend to strip out of their body-hugging wetsuits right on the edge of the road for all the world . . . I mean the sparkling azure-blue ocean is beautiful as it stretches out into eternity.

You know, once the June Gloom clears.

As Anne drove out the exit, she waved to the driver of the incoming car. We all recognized the vehicle immediately, but the crazy part was seeing that Hope was behind the wheel. She was finally allowed to drive the family car with her peers as passengers. (It's a silly California law.) Don't ever let her know that I said she was riding with her peers, because she was actually with her stepsisters.

I couldn't tell if the sour expression on her face was because of the steps, the fact that Sam and I were standing near Drew, or the car itself. See, the car was purchased while Hope was out of the country, so she didn't get any say in it. She was *supposed* to be involved in the decision, but her stepmom had decided that her own daughters shouldn't have to wait a minute longer for the car Hope's dad was paying for. The result: a customized pink-and-purple Mini Cooper with a silver diamond etched on the roof, sparkly pink spinners on the wheels, and purple fur-covered seats. Not exactly subtle.

My excitement over seeing Hope behind the wheel of the car was tempered by the fact that she stepped out in full on Goth-Ick mode. That's what she calls her style of dress and the attitude that goes with it. As she squeezed out of the driver's seat, I saw she was sporting a full-on Victorian-style outfit complete with high-necked black lace top and a long black skirt. While it was certainly a good choice for a chilly June Gloomy morning, I couldn't help but think she'd eventually grow to regret it come afternoon when the clouds burned off and the sun came shining out. The ensemble was topped by a black blazer with a violently red rose sewn on the sleeve, which, if I'm not mistaken—and I'm not—was dripping embroidered blood from the petals.

Talk about wearing your heart on your sleeve. And in her eyes as well. As she approached, I could see she was wearing a pair of her bloodiest red contacts. Hope changes eye colors like other girls change shoes.

Hope pushed past us, grabbing Sam's arm and pulling her along.

Ouch. If anyone could kill with her eyes, it would be Hope. She wasn't even aiming at me, but I got hit with the shrapnel on that one.

I hung back to give Sam some time to work the poison from Hope's eyes . . . which left me alone with Drew, Eric, and the steps.

"She's been at Hope-times-ten all morning," Belinda said as we watched Hope try to wrench the locked doors open.

"Word to the wise," Alexis said. "Never get in a car with someone going through a breakup." Then, she actually clasped her hand over her mouth as if she had forgotten that Drew was the one Hope was in the process of breaking up with.

Nice.

Alexis and Belinda are the least identical, identical twins I've ever met. Not to say that they don't look exactly alike, because they do. But they do everything in their power not to. Belinda is all earth tones and shades of white. She prefers flowing dresses and outfits that complement her long blond hair. On the other hand, Alexis prefers loud colors in her clothes, and the tighter the better. Her hair is chopped short and at odd angles that cost a couple hundred dollars at the trendiest salon on Sunset Boulevard. Even at eight thirty in the morning, Alexis was made up for a night on the town, while I've never seen Belinda in anything more than a thin layer of foundation and muted lip gloss.

Guess which one got to pick the custom design of their car.

The one thing truly identical about them is they have the exact same shade of natural honey-blond hair. And they both make Mary-Kate and Ashley look fat. Hence why we've nick-named them the Twin Twigs of Terror.

"But don't worry," Alexis added, moving closer to the guys who weren't me. "We're totally on Team Drew."

"Alexis," Belinda whispered loudly with a glance in my direction. Like I was going to run and tell Hope what she'd said. Like Hope would even care. Or be surprised.

"What?" Alexis said with mock innocence. "It's a fact of the world we live in today. Everyone has to pick a side. Have we learned nothing from our celebrity friends?"

Now, here's the difference between us and them. If me and my friends had ever said something like that, we'd be going for sarcastic. Alexis was being genuine.

Even though their styles are night and day, Alexis and Belinda are of one mind on the critical subjects affecting the world: the importance of fashion, the power of celebrity, and, most important, the entertainment value of scandal. Which is exactly why they were best friends with the girl in the silver Lexus hybrid SUV careening its way into the parking lot.

Now that I think of it, *friends* may not be the most accurate term; *followers* might be more appropriate . . . or *minions*. Even better. Minions it is.

The driver tore up to the front of the lot, parking diagonally across two spots. This was not a real problem since most of the parking lot would be empty, but it was still rude, if you ask me.

The SUV door swung open, and out came a pair of legs that had all the soccer guys—and a few of the male Drama Geeks—swiveling to look. It wasn't like they hadn't seen those legs before, but being that it was summer there was slightly more leg to see than during the school year. They were the legs of a girl that had dressed in anticipation of the warm sunny day that would eventually evolve from the gray morning mess.

They were the legs of Holly Mayflower.

Twice as talented and countless times more evil than her older sister, Heather, Holly Mayflower had been out of school for most of last semester working on a sitcom pilot. The show got picked up, but Holly did not. She returned to Orion in disgrace and driving a new SUV her father bought to soften the blow.

Holly likes to think of herself as an actress–singer–model–movie mogul in the making. I guess, technically, she is all those things, but I prefer to think of her as a Queen Bee–wannabe TV star–mean girl–daddy's girl who knows how to use her influence to get what she wants. That may be one of the more convoluted hyphenates I've ever put down on paper, but it fits her to a baby-doll T.

Oh, the hyphenate thing? That's how we distinguish people in Los Angeles. The more hyphens, the more success-ful you are, I guess. Me? I'm an actor-photographer (well, part-time photographer) still in search of my ultimate success and further hyphens.

Holly is just a smidge over one year younger than her sister, Heather. I guess their mom wanted to get all the "unsightly" baby weight out of the way all at once. Heather and Holly: As the story goes, their mother had named them after flowers, in honor of their Mayflower last name. Too bad nobody told the woman that Heather and Holly aren't so much flowers as they are shrubs.

Holly got big hugs from Alexis and Belinda, as if they hadn't seen each other for years, instead of hours. Then she read the awkwardness on all of our faces and turned to see Hope and Sam off by the entrance.

"This is the problem with being fashionably on time," Holly said with a practiced flip of her red hair. She then looked right at Eric and added, "You miss all the good stuff."

Eric cleared his throat. "Good morning, Holly."

"It *is*, isn't it?" She gave another pointed look over toward Hope and Sam. "Or is it? Flying solo?"

"What?" Eric asked. "No. Sam? No."

"Oh," she said. "I thought Drew might have inspired you to . . . know what? Never mind. My mistake." Yeah. Like Holly ever makes mistakes.

She smiled and sauntered off with her minions. As they walked away, all the guys in the area were watching Holly's form-fitting shorts as they hugged her perfectly sculpted butt. Hell, even I was looking.

Once I snapped out of the hypnotic rhythm of her strut, I realized that I was alone with Eric and Drew once again. No matter how much I try, I guess they're destined to be a part of my life.

We were saved from any further awkwardness by the arrival of Mr. Randall, the drama teacher. He let us all into school and then went to open up the gym for the soccer team.

"Holly's in pure form this morning," I said as I joined up with Sam and Hope.

"That's about the only thing pure about her," Sam said.

I turned to Hope. "You okay?"

She cocked her head to the side and shrugged.

"If you need anything," I added.

She nodded and then pointed toward her locker. "I'm gonna . . ."

"We'll meet you back here," Sam said as we turned and headed off in the opposite direction toward our lockers.

"What was that?" I asked.

"I wish I knew," Sam said. "She was like that when I tried to talk to her yesterday, too."

"That's . . . weird."

"I know."

Don't get me wrong. I understood that Hope was going through a breakup and all, but this was different. She'd never been quiet before. The shrugging and the pointing . . . that was just not like her. Yelling and screaming and railing at everyone in the vicinity? That's the Hope we all know and fear. Silent Hope was just . . . unnerving.

No other breakup had ever led Hope to dress in full-on Victorian Matron before either. She looked like she was mourning someone's death. I only hoped the outfit wasn't foreshadowing.

"She won't even tell me what the fight was about," Sam added. "Drew won't tell Eric either."

"Did you ever think that they're not saying anything because they don't want you and Eric talking about them behind their backs?"

"We're their best friends," Sam insisted. "That's what we're supposed to do."

I guess I couldn't argue with that. I spend a fair amount of time talking about Sam behind her back too. . . . Wait. That doesn't sound right.

"I'm worried," Sam said.

I nodded. I was a little worried myself.

We walked the rest of the way to our brand-spanking-new lockers in a contemplative silence. The lockers were the price Heather Mayflower's father had paid to ensure that his daughter still graduated after she had sabotaged the Spring Theatrical Production of *The Wizard of Oz*. Ignoring all the drama that she had caused, it did result in a pretty cool repercussion.

The lockers were totally tricked out. They were twice the size of our old lockers and had electronic combinations that we could program ourselves. I punched in my combo (2-4-6-0-1) and dropped my lunch in the cooler—a nice little add-on to keep our hot food hot and our cool food cool. With the inlaid mirrors, voice recorders for leaving personal messages, and air fresheners, I'd consider moving in if they were a tad larger.

When Anthony Mayflower makes up for his children's mistakes, he goes big. He probably would have upgraded to lockers with refrigerators and microwaves if the school could have afforded to pay the electric bill.

"So how are we going to do it?" Sam asked as she closed her locker.

"Do what?"

"Get them back together?"

Oh, dear.

This was not good. Sam had that scheming look in her eyes. That always meant trouble. Sam isn't the schemer. *I'm* the schemer. Sam usually goes along—unwillingly—with my plans. Our success rate is somewhere around fifty-four percent, slightly better than average, but still fairly sucky. In the end my schemes usually work out, but that doesn't mean we don't wind up trapped inside the school observatory at some point along the way. Sam's plans have even less of a success rate, if you can imagine.

"You're kidding, right?"

"Nope. We're going to rekindle their relationship."

"And what makes you think they *want* it rekindled?"

"You saw Hope this morning," Sam said. "She's miserable. And not the fun kind of miserable act she usually puts on to scare people. This is serious."

I had to agree. I had never seen Hope like this before. But I wasn't entirely sure that getting back together with Drew was the answer. Then again, they did seem to enjoy breaking up and making up in their relationship. They certainly did it often enough.

"As Hope's best friends," Sam continued, "we owe it to her to do everything in our power to make sure that she gives her relationship every chance at surviving."

Thank you, Dr. Phil. "Hope is *not* going to like us getting involved."

She crossed the hall to give me a light tap on the cheek. "Silly boy," she said. "We're not going to *tell* her."

Miss Julie

"I'm dying to hear what you've got in mind," I lied as we walked toward the Saundra Hall Auditorium (or Hall Hall as we like to call it). I kept my voice low as various class-mates were hurrying past so they could get a good seat for our first day. I also kept an eye out for Hope because she was the last one I wanted to overhear us. "I'm guessing it's very *Parent Trap*. But the question is are we going with the Hayley Mills or the Lindsay Lohan pre-party-girl version?"

"It's going to be intricate," she said. "Nothing subtle for Hope."

"Will it have multiple phases? Please tell me there will be multiple phases."

"And maybe even a contingency plan or two."

I have to admit . . . I was getting excited. Summer in Malibu can get kind of boring. I mean, think about it. We live in a beautiful beach community with almost perfect weather all year long. Manipulating Hope's life could provide for some entertainment.

Okay, seriously folks. I was worried about the girl. It was possible that she and Drew were meant to be together. I mean, some people like to fight. Isn't that what we've learned from TV and movies over the years? Fighting couples are overcompensating for sexual tension and all that? Not that I ever noticed any sexual tension between Hope and Drew, but I was no expert on these things. Just because I wasn't so sure they were destined to be together didn't mean that they weren't. I've been known to be wrong before. Once or twice.

Besides, what harm could we really do? Hope was leaving for New York in two weeks.

Hope silently fell into step with us as we entered Hall Hall. While we had been at our lockers, most of the rest of the Drama Geeks had filtered into the theater. Students from the sophomore, junior, and senior classes were all mingling together, which was cool. During the school year our classes were broken up by grade so we only worked together on the spring show. This was a chance for everyone to mix things up.

There were quite a number of people sitting almost at the front of the house. Odd that nobody ever wants to be in the first row. It's the same way in the classroom too. Following Hope's lead, we walked right up and filled in a trio of seats in the empty row. I guess she figured everyone would be staring at her anyway. Might as well make it easier on them.

I decided to look back at them as well.

Jason MacMillan was a few rows back, looking depressed.

I suspect that his mood had something to do with his relationship recently passing its expiration date. For the past few years, he had been dating a girl in the grade above us. When his girlfriend, Wren, graduated and went off to film a music video and then attend an early summer session at college, they had decided to call it quits without even bothering to try the long-distance thing. It was like couples were breaking up all over the place lately. I wondered if Sam might take some inspiration from that.

I caught Jason's sad eyes focused in our direction, but he quickly turned away when he saw me looking. It was possible his sad act was just an act and he was already scoping out Hope for a possible entanglement. The only problem with that idea was that his eyes had seemed to be directed toward Sam.

The usual suspects were scattered about the rows behind us too. Tasha Valentine, Goth girl, was sitting off by herself, lost in a world of Emo Rock coming from her 80-gig video iPod. (It was either that or she was listening to the audiobook of *The House at Pooh Corner*. With Tasha, you could go either way.) And of course, our stage manager extra-unordinaire, Jimmy Wilkey, was flitting about the place setting things up. Meanwhile, Holly was holding court over Alexis and Belinda as well as a collection of junior girls who fancied themselves as modern-day Pink Ladies prepping to rule the school once Holly was gone the same time next year.

Mr. Randall, our drama teacher, came out from backstage with a strange woman beside him. (Not that there was anything unusual about her. I just mean we didn't recognize her.)

He stepped up to the edge of the stage and cleared his throat dramatically, which was wholly unnecessary as we were already quiet. Strangers do that to us. It's not that we're afraid of them or anything. Seeing strangers at our school makes us incredibly curious. Where other kids might whisper about who she was, we tend to be much more patient gossips at Orion. We knew that we'd find out soon enough. *Then* the gossiping would begin about what a person like her was doing at our school.

"Welcome back," Mr. Randall said. "It's been ages." It had actually been four days. No one laughed since Mr. Randall has opened all the Summer Theatrical Programs of the past few years with that same lame joke. Not even the ninth graders—who, I guess, were now tenth graders—found it funny. And it was totally new to them.

"Okay," he said. "I need new material. As you all know, we've got a fun two-week program ahead of us. But, what you don't know is how much fun it's going to be. I know we usually spend this time doing our impression of Mickey and Judy putting on a show in the barn, but this summer we have a different agenda in store."

Mr. Randall paused while the whispers began. The less-theatrically aware of my peers were wondering who the heck Mickey and Judy were and where this barn was located. (*Aside:* He was referring to Mickey Rooney and Judy Garland, who used to costar in movies where their characters almost always wound up putting on an impromptu musical in whatever arena was available to them—usually a barn.)

"This year," he continued, "instead of taking our two weeks to put on a no-budget show, we're going to change things up a bit and focus on scene work. The first week of the program we're going to work on monologues, while the second week will be all about group scenes."

That announcement was met with a chorus of groans. I guess after the debacle that was *The Wizard of Oz*, people were looking to put on a real show. Even one that we only took two weeks to put together. Personally, I kind of liked the idea of doing real scene work. We usually spend so much time getting ready for whatever show we're working on that we don't always get to work the basics of acting during the school year *or* in the summer program.

"I know, I know," Mr. Randall said in reaction to the groans. "It's all about the show. But how about if I sweeten the deal?" This is one of the things that really drives me crazy about Orion. Mr. Randall is our teacher. He's trying to teach us a valuable lesson. But the only way he can get away with making us do something we don't want to do is by bribing us. I would have called him on it, but first I wanted to know what he had to offer.

"Ladies and gentlemen," he continued. "I would like to introduce Ms. Julie Blackstone." Mr. Randall gave a sweep of his hand in his guest's direction. The beautiful, dark-haired stranger walked to the edge of the stage. Talk about an entrance. It was even more impressive that she had been standing there the whole time.

"Call me Julie," she said.

"Actually," Mr. Randall said. "Call her Ms. Blackstone." He turned to her to explain. "It's a school rule that the students have to address faculty formally."

"Okay," she said with a smile. "Call me Miss Julie."

Most of us laughed at the reference.

(*Aside: Miss Julie* is a play by August Strindberg. The joke wasn't that funny. I think we were overcompensating so the pretty lady would like us.)

Mr. Randall continued, "As you all know, Ms. Monroe is off on her honeymoon right now. And Ms. Blackstone—"

"Miss Julie."

"Ms. *Blackstone*," he insisted. "Will be taking her place."

In a story that could have been titled "Love Among the Arts," Ms. Monroe, our music teacher–assistant director–not quite old maid recently tied the knot with Orion Academy's art teacher-graphic designer-confirmed bachelor, Mr. Telasco. They had waited all through the school year to have their wedding. Rather than postpone things until after the summer program, Ms. Monroe (she kept her name) decided to go on her honeymoon immediately. Can't say I blame her.

We had all been wondering how Mr. Randall was going to get through the program without her. Working with all us Drama Geeks from nine to three every day for two weeks could cause anyone to have a breakdown. Enter our answer: the oddly familiar Ms. Blackstone.

And then, it hit me.

Blackstone.

"Urp!" I said. It was not a pleasant sound. Or one that I had intended to make at all, but the realization hit me so fast that I reacted . . . and at a surprisingly loud volume. I slid down in my chair as Sam and Hope busied themselves by acting like they didn't know me.

"Sounds like someone's made the connection," Ms. Blackstone . . . I'm sorry, *Miss Julie*, said.

"Yes," Mr. Randall nodded with a laugh. "I believe someone has. For those of you a step behind, Ms. Blackstone is the daughter of Hartley Blackstone. She's student teaching with us this summer *and* she has a very exciting announcement to make."

"Hi," Ms. Blackstone said, throwing in a friendly wave. I would much prefer if the school policy would allow us to call her Julie since "Ms. Blackstone" was only a couple years older than us seniors. I decided to go with calling her Miss Julie, like she'd said . . . if only for the fact that it is was technically against school rules.

"I hate being . . . well . . . this is going to sound pretentious, but does everyone know who my father is?" she asked.

Duh!

A sea of bobbing heads nodded yes.

Hartley Blackstone is one of the most famous producer-director-actor-writer-songwriter-choreographers (a quintuple hyphenate!) in Broadway history. He's won a Tony Award in just about every category you can win a Tony Award except costume design. (I hear he's working on completing his set by designing the wardrobe for his next production.)

Which begged the question: What in the *world* was his

daughter doing at Orion Academy? Shouldn't she be at some amazing art school in New York? London? *Anywhere* else?

"I guess you've heard of Dad," she said. Even Alexis and Belinda—who really had no right to be there in the first place—knew who her father was. "Okay, so here's the deal," she continued. "I've got to do the student teaching thing for summer credits. This is all kind of last minute on account of . . . well, let me give you guys a tip: Never jet off to your dad's London premiere without locking in your course schedule first. School bureaucrats can be such a bitch." We were hanging on every word. "So, if I want to get my degree, I've got to complete this little two-week unit and then quietly graduate before anyone starts asking questions." At about this point, I believe Mr. Randall's head was about as close to exploding as it had been during the spring show. "So, I bribed my way into this program—"

"Actually," Mr. Randall interrupted. "We were in dire need of another teacher, and Ms. Blackstone kindly offered to help out."

"That's what I said," she added with a smile. "And since things were dire all around, *Ms. Blackstone* wasn't about to throw things to chance and arranged it all with a little help from Daddy. You've all heard about the Hartley Blackstone Acting School, right?"

Sam nearly ripped the arms of her chair off the metal frame. That would be a *yes*. The Blackstone Acting School is a summer theater program in which Blackstone only accepts the most talented students from all over the world to attend.

It's nearly impossible to get into. So much so that no one I know has even tried.

"He's left two open spots this year," she continued. "For one girl and one boy from Orion Academy. And Dad's going to come and pick them himself."

There was an explosion of voices as everyone started talking at once. I didn't know what Sam was saying to me. I wasn't even sure what I was saying to her. All I did know was that I've never seen the Drama Geeks that excited before in my life. And we're talking about a fairly melodramatic group of people to begin with.

In the midst of the excitement, Hope remained sitting quietly, as she had been all morning. If anything, I would have thought that this announcement would have gotten some kind of reaction out of her. The rest of us, however, were reacting all over the place.

Eventually, Mr. Randall managed to get us back under some semblance of control. "It's going to work like this. You'll have all week to prepare one monologue for Mr. Blackstone. He'll be here on Friday to watch you perform. He'll give you what I can only assume will be valuable notes on your acting that you can take and apply to your scenes. Then, next Friday he'll come back to see your group scenes and make his final decision."

This time, there was no outburst, but you could feel the energy in the room. We were about to explode again. It was only a matter of time.

"I could continue talking," Mr. Randall said, "but you guys

aren't really hearing anything right now, anyway. So why don't we take a break and you can pick groups for your scenes."

Pandemonium.

That's the only word that can be used to describe the auditorium. As theater students we can be overly exuberant when we're just greeting one another in the morning, but give us something like this—an opportunity to study under one of the masters of theater?

Watch. Out.

I immediately turned to Sam and Hope. "What scene are we going to do?"

And was met with silence.

"Hello? Anybody home?"

Okay, I get that they were a little stunned. Hope was going through a lot at the moment. And Sam . . . she probably never expected to have this kind of opportunity back when she was going to a poorly funded public school. But everyone was teaming up around us. We had to move fast if we wanted to round out our group with someone who knew stage left from stage right.

"Anyone looking for a fourth?" Jason MacMillan asked as he pushed his way past some overeager sophomore girls who, I think, wanted him to join their group as much for his stellar acting ability as his good looks.

Sam finally came out of her coma. "Yes!" she said with a little more excitement than I had expected. "You *so* have to join us."

"Great," he said, grabbing a seat beside Sam.

"Great," she said, looking relieved.

"Great," I said . . . suspiciously.

Okay, maybe I was overreacting, but Sam seemed way more excited to team with Jason than she did when it was just Hope and me. Jason is an incredibly talented actor. Let's be honest, he was the real competition for the guys. I wasn't deluded enough to think that it was going to be easy beating out Jason for the spot. I'd need to ace my audition just to be considered along with him. Still, it wasn't like I was going to bring Sam down or anything.

"Are you guys already teamed up?" a hesitant voice asked from beside me. I looked up to see Gary McNulty leaning over my seat. It was weird that he sounded so shy since Gary's usually quite the outgoing fellow. He played the head flying monkey in *The Wizard of Oz*. People are still talking about the aerial somersault he spontaneously threw in during the show.

"Sorry, Monkey Boy," I said. "Thirty seconds too late. I think we're full up." As much as I would have liked Gary on the team, any more than four people would seriously cut into our stage time. I could see that Sam and Jason were with me because they were solemnly nodding in agreement. Hope was still looking down at her lap.

"Oh, okay," he said as he walked off. It was a shame there wasn't room for one more. Gary was one of the best actors in the junior class. He was also pretty cute with his curly brown hair and thin silver-frame glasses. Not that I noticed.

I didn't really have time to dwell more on these thoughts, because something much more interesting was sashaying up to us. Holly and the Anorexettes were making their way across the aisle.

This should be good.

"Jason," Holly said as she leaned over me, Hope, and Sam to get to him. "Tell me you haven't already found a group."

My, aren't we the popular foursome?

"Sorry," he said. "But I'm on Sam's team."

Um . . . when did we become *Sam's* team?

Holly gave Sam a look that could quite possibly be described as a sneer. "If you change your mind," she said, "I've got something special in mind for our scene."

"I'm sure you do," Sam said. Her defenses were already raised in ways that Holly's sister, Heather, never managed to evoke from her.

Hope finally looked like she had some life in her. Girl could smell a fight from a mile away. Not that the pending battle was nearly that distant. "Don't go thinking about knocking out the competition like Heather did on *Wizard*," Hope warned softly, but firmly. "I'm watching you."

"I don't need to rely on tricks like my sister," Holly said, "I've got actual talent. More than enough to earn me this spot in Blackstone's program."

With that, she and the twigs turned and stalked off in search of an innocent victim. The worst part about our little exchange was that Holly was right. She does have talent. I was just glad that, being male, I didn't have to go up against her.

On the other hand . . . I looked to my best friend.

"Well," Sam said, "now I *have* to win."

Oh boy.

A Lie of the Mind

Hope and I were among the first to get to the Kenneth Graham Pavilion, which is the Orion Academy version of a lunchroom. It's actually a covered outdoor patio with no lunch-making facilities at all, but a beautiful view of the Pacific Ocean. The sun had finally burned through the clouds. It was shaping up to be a pleasant and warm day.

Hope took off her jacket as we grabbed a table nearest the ocean view. The rest of the Drama Geeks quickly came in behind us, staking out spots for themselves and their scene partners.

The soccer guys hadn't arrived for lunch yet, which was just as well, considering I would be useless trying to deflect Hope and Drew on my own. Sam had stayed behind in Hall Hall with Jason to pump Mr. Randall full of questions about the auditions. Since I knew Sam would fill me in on all that she had learned, I figured I didn't need to hang around. Besides, I was hungry.

What I didn't realize was that this would leave me alone with Hope for the first time since her breakup with Drew.

Don't get me wrong. Hope and I are really close. Not quite as close as Sam and me, but I still consider Hope one of my best friends. It's just . . . we don't do *serious* well. We don't have heart-to-hearts. Ever.

"So . . . ," I said.

She didn't even bother to look up. Not that I blamed her. I wasn't giving her much to work with.

I tried a new approach. "If you ever want to talk about you and Drew."

"I don't."

"Oh, no . . . I get that," I said. "It's just . . . I know a thing or two about how Drew can dump on people."

"Who said he dumped me?"

"No. I meant . . . I didn't . . ."

Hence why she and I don't do this often. We kind of suck at it.

Hope looked at me with her big red eyes, softening. "I'm sorry. I'm tired. I was up all night, writing."

"Let's see." I grabbed her notebook and started flipping through the pages.

"Not there," she said, pulling her necklace out from her shirt and dangling it in front of me. That meant she had been doing serious writing. Her notebook is for her fun writing; really crappy poems in honor of her dog that died five years ago. She calls it *The Book of the Dead Puppy Poetry*. She's already on volume six. But her serious work . . . *that* she keeps safely locked in a flash drive tied to a silk rope around her neck. The work in there is deep and meaningful and she only shows it to friends on rare occasions. Somehow, I didn't think this was going to be one of those times.

"That bad?" I asked.

"It's just Drew . . . he's hopeless."

"Literally," I said, trying to break the mood with my usual bad pun.

Hope didn't even crack a smile. At the very least, I had expected her to kick me under the table for making light of her pain. But nothing. No response whatsoever. Thankfully, we were saved from further discomfort when Sam and Jason arrived.

"Learn anything good?" I asked.

Sam dropped her lunch on the table and took a seat next to me. "Not really. Mr. Randall is staying pretty mum on things so he doesn't get our hopes up."

"Too late," Jason and I said.

"Should we get to work?" Sam asked, scanning the room. "Everyone else is."

The pavilion was abuzz with activity. I guess the soccer team's morning practice was running late because the guys were still nowhere in sight. That was fine by me. We did have work to do. Besides, I wasn't ready to see Eric go through the King Solomon task of deciding who to eat with. If he sat with Drew, that meant he wouldn't be sitting with us. There was no way one poor little cafeteria table could handle the tension of Hope and Drew at the same table. But I couldn't see Eric blowing off Sam either. He'd sat with her (and us) for lunch almost every single day since they'd started dating.

Unbelievable. I actually felt bad for Eric. Welcome to Bizarro World.

Without the soccer guys to get in the way, the drama students had broken up into teams and spread out across the cafeteria. I imagine the same discussion was taking place at every table.

First, we were eyeing the competition.

"I feel bad for Tasha," I said. "She's stuck with Jimmy."

"Girl needs to be more aggressive," Hope said. "That is exactly what happens when you sit back and let the world dictate your life. You get stuck with Jimmy Wilkey and a tenth-grade munchkin."

Just to note, she wasn't insulting the tenth grader by calling her a munchkin. Back when we did *Wizard* and they were ninth graders, they played munchkins. Which is just to say that they only had a couple lines in the play and haven't really acted on our stage before. Jimmy's never acted before either. He usually zips around as stage manager making sure Mr. Randall has everything he needs whether or not he wants it.

After *Wizard* Jimmy got on this kick about learning all aspects of theater to make him a better stage manager, and he asked Mr. Randall if he could try out acting in the summer program. Not that he needed to ask, but it would be against Jimmy's programming to tell Mr. Randall he wanted to do anything. Who knew? Maybe Jimmy would surprise us all with his hidden talents.

Honestly? I wasn't holding out hope.

And neither was Hope, for that matter.

"Didn't see that one coming," Jason said as his eyes turned in the direction of Holly Mayflower and the twigs. They were sitting with Gary McNulty.

"Holly and Monkey Boy?" I asked. I would have thought that he'd team with his best friend, Madison, but it's possible Holly made him an offer . . . he'd come to regret.

"Makes sense," Sam said as she took out her lunch. "Once you harness his natural exuberance, he's actually pretty good. I probably would've gone with him too . . . if I didn't have you guys, I mean."

I looked at Hope to see if she thought she was being insulted too, but she was busy glaring at her stepsisters so I just put it out of my mind. In this world, I've learned that you can choose to read something into everything a person says or just ignore it and assume they meant it in the best way possible. I prefer to go the positive route . . . but keep on alert, just in case I'm being insulted behind my back. Not that Sam would ever intentionally insult my acting, but there was a fair amount of hesitation on her part when we were choosing sides—I mean *teams*—earlier. Then again, maybe I was being overly sensitive. That's often a problem for us creative types.

"I say we go with Shakespeare," Jason said, moving the discussion past the gossiping-about-our-competition stage.

"Isn't that a little obvious?" I asked. *Everyone* would be doing Shakespeare.

"You'd prefer something in the absurdist oeuvre?" Sam asked. "Perhaps some *Waiting for Godot?*"

"Shakespeare it is," I said. Sam knew full well how I felt about absurdist theater, and especially *Godot*.

(*Aside:* I'm sorry. I know it's like supposed to be this work of genius and all, but I just don't get it. The play has no real plot beyond these two freaks waiting around by a tree for some guy named Godot to show up. And he never shows! That's it. Nothing happens! Sorry if I just spoiled the ending, but we're not talking about the mystery of *Lost* here. Everyone who goes to the play already knows what they're getting into from the start. And yet they *still* go to see it!)

"What play do you think we should do?" I asked. "Nothing too obvious."

"Gee, how about *Romeo and Juliet*," Jason said.

The three of us stared at him. Blankly.

"That was a joke," he said. "You should have known that by the fact that I said 'Gee.' Do I ever talk like that?"

"Oh," Sam and I said with a tremendous amount of relief.

"Okay," Jason said, sounding a little hurt that we all missed the joke. "I was thinking more like *Measure for Measure* or *Troilus and Cressida*."

"I'd prefer comedy," Hope said with no measure of jovial attitude in her tone at all.

"Yeah, we can tell," Sam said. "Technically, *Measure for Measure* is a comedy."

"Really?" I asked. "A play about a man demanding that a nun sleep with him to save her imprisoned brother is considered a comedy?"

"By some," Sam said.

"Yeah. We won't be doing that one," I said.

"How about *Twelfth Night?*" Hope suggested, showing her first signs of enthusiasm for the scene.

"Mistaken identity comedy about an identical twin brother and sister," I said. "Sounds perfect for us." We were all familiar with the play already since we'd studied it for a week in English sophomore year. There were a bunch of good characters in it, so I was pretty sure that there'd be some good scenes. "Agreed?"

"Agreed," Sam said.

That left Jason.

"Works for me," he said. "We can figure out which scene later. Now we should choose our monologues since those come first."

Hope and I looked at each other. "We'll save that for later," I said, trying to head off any discussion. I've tried to pick monologues with Sam before. It's not a fun time. She can be somewhat . . . indecisive about these things. To the point where I swear I've seen smoke coming out of her ears because her mind was working so fast at going over all the options.

"The guys are here," Sam said as the soccer team filed into the pavilion. I suspect she said this to prepare Hope for whatever choice Eric—and by default, Drew—made about where to sit.

We all sat in breathless anticipation as we watched the guys file in.

Okay, actually, Sam was the only one holding her breath. I was breathing quite regularly. I figured either nothing was going to happen or we'd get a fun show to go along with our lunch. Jason, on the other hand, wasn't even aware that anything was going on. He had his own breakup issues to work through, anyway. Hope, however, was very pointedly breathing in a relaxed manner. She was sitting with her back to the door and hadn't bothered to turn to watch the guys come in. It was all an act, though. I could see her nonchalantly watching Sam's face for a reaction.

All conversation stopped in our group as the soccer guys found their own empty tables or joined their drama friends. Nobody came near us, knowing better than to look like they were taking Hope's side. The soccer team and Drama Geeks usually blend together rather well—especially the soccer guys and drama *girls*—but we were apparently personae non grata. It was only day one and already people were taking sides.

Great.

They arrived in clumps at first, all hot and sweaty from practice. And I have to say, I didn't much mind them not joining us. Hope's eyes continued to flick up to see Sam's reaction. But Sam remained stoic, going with neutral since she knew she was being watched.

After the initial rush, things slowed down and the guys were entering in pairs with some distance between them. With every new flash of uniform that came around the corner, I watched Sam's eyes register who it was, then focus on her food. It was quite the performance. She was giving nothing away.

Soon, there were longer gaps between the guys as the

stragglers followed. One by one and two by two they found their seats. The noise level had increased in the pavilion, but we were still pretty quiet at our table. Eventually, the stream of guys slowed to the point of stopping. And still, no Drew and Eric.

When it finally became clear that they weren't coming, Sam simply leaned over and took a bite out of her PB and J. I turned to nonchalantly gauge Hope's reaction. "Crestfallen" would be a good way to describe it. Though I wasn't sure if she was sorry that she didn't have a chance to *see* Drew or to *fight* with him.

"Who wants to hit the library after school to pick up some monologues?" Hope asked. Clearly she was in a distraught state if she was going to suggest going with Sam to pick out monologues.

"Can't," Sam said, with her eyes trained on me. "We have plans."

I had no idea what Sam was talking about, but since I had done the same thing to her many times before I just nodded my head like I agreed.

"Doing what?" Hope asked, looking directly at me.

Oh, how I love being put on the spot. Hope knew that Sam and I told her everything that we were up to. The fact that Sam was referring to some ambiguous "plans" instead of just saying what those "plans" were meant she was probably hiding something. Now it was up to me to come up with an excuse or Hope wouldn't trust us. And it couldn't be any old excuse. It had to be believable. Also, important enough that we couldn't postpone it, but not so important that it would be suspicious that we hadn't mentioned it to Hope before. But, most of all, we had to be doing something that Hope couldn't invite herself along for.

This was a lot to ask for in a lie. And while I'm pretty comfortable with the whole lying thing, I've never been particularly good at improv.

"We're helping Mom with a private showing," I said, surprising both Sam *and* me in the process. "Some Beverly Hills trophy wife wants an entire wardrobe for her dog that matches the purses she carries him in. You're welcome to join us, if you want."

"Oh," Hope said. "That's okay." I wasn't sure if she believed me, but she wasn't going to call me on it, either. She'd gone to a few of these private showings before and was miserable every time. I usually try to drag a friend along because they're incredibly time consuming and totally boring to sit through on my own. First, we have to dress up a couple dozen stuffed dogs in samples of Mom's entire line of doggy wardrobe. Then lug them all to the client's house and pull a Vanna White showing off the designs while the client criticizes everything from the color to the fit to the thread count. Hope nearly lost it the last time she went with us when the client asked if we thought an outfit made her Chihuahua look fat.

Seriously.

Sam had this satisfied look on her face, clearly glad that we had pulled that one off. But I was more curious about what she had going on in that head of hers. What did she really have in mind for our afternoon? And did I want to have any part of it?

A Delicate Balance

Sam and I watched as Hope squeezed her extralarge breasts into the Mini Cooper and tore out of the parking lot. Alexis and Belinda were hitting the beach with Holly, so they were off in her hybrid. The soccer team had already cut out about a half hour before us. It wasn't long before Sam and I were the last ones in the parking lot.

I started Electra and waited for the purr of her engine. We always had a moment of silence before we took off, both to appreciate the fact that the car was running and to listen for any telltale signs that she might change her mind and go dead on us. I don't know much about fixing cars, but when you own a classic, you have to at least know what to listen for.

Everything sounded good.

I put my hand on the gearshift. "Where are we going?"

"Turn right out of the parking lot."

Electra remained in park. "Well, obviously," I said. Going

left on Breakwater Lane would take us to a dead end. Literally. We'd go off a cliff.

"I'll direct you," Sam said with a bigger smile than I'd ever seen on her face. Sam's ability to hide things from me is only second to her ability to scheme. Which is my way of saying she can't do either with any discernable talent.

Electra continued to idle. On the bright side, the engine sounded pretty good. "Is there a reason you don't want to tell me where we're going?"

"Because if I tell you, you might not want to go."

"I don't want to go already," I said.

"We're going to get some coffee," Sam said with her gaze focused intently out the passenger side window. What had her attention, I did not know. I assumed she was more interested in looking *away* from something—namely me—than looking *at* something—namely air.

By that point, I was able to put two and two together and come up with something. "The coffeehouse at Malibu Colony Plaza?"

Sam nodded her head.

I rolled my eyes.

The Colony is a quaint little shopping center by the beach. The shops run the gamut from a really nice supermarket to upscale boutiques to a newspaper stand and Subway sandwich shop. It may be small, but it's the place to be and be seen running your daily errands. The Colony gets more celebrity sightings per day than the reception desk at the Wonderland Rehab Center.

It's also across the street from Eric Whitman's Malibu Dream House.

"So, we're meeting Eric," I said as I put Electra in drive. "What's the big deal?"

"I didn't know how you'd feel about discussing Hope and Drew with him," Sam said. "Since you guys have issues or whatever."

"We don't have *issues*," I said. "We just both want to be the only man in your life. Me, platonically, of course. Him . . . well, I think we both know what he wants. Seems to me, you're the one with the issues."

"Funny."

"Look, I don't really have any problems with Eric anymore," I said. "He's never going to be my best friend, but he's your boyfriend. I can deal." And I *could* deal. We had been hanging out together for more than a month without incident. I couldn't figure out why it was such a big deal all of a sudden.

The reason hit me at about the same time we hit the Pacific Coast Highway. We'd never been a trio. Someone had always been with us. Usually two someones: Drew and Hope. And since Suze had been tagging along we'd been a right jolly old gang. But now, with me as the third wheel, we were about to enter a new dynamic entirely.

I could see why she was nervous.

A few miles up the PCH, I turned Electra into the Malibu Colony Plaza and found a spot near the coffeehouse. Thankfully, it was still early in the season. Give it a week or two and the parking lot would be packed with cars filled with tourists hoping for a celeb sighting in the frozen food aisle of the supermarket.

Before we got out of Electra, I flipped on my cell phone to see if I'd missed any calls or anything. I get lousy reception in Malibu, especially at school.

"Suze made it to New York safely," I said, reading her text. "Hey. If we get the spots in Blackstone's program we'll be able to spend the summer hanging out with her in the city. And Hope will be there too."

"And Eric will be a short train ride to the Hamptons," Sam added.

"Oh," I said. "Guess you figured that one out already."

"Yep."

What can I say? Sometimes I'm a little slow. So, in addition to this audition being for one of the best acting programs in the country, Sam had the added stress of being able to spend the summer a train ride away from her boyfriend or being stuck on the other side of the country from him. Yeah. It was going to be a fun week.

We made our way to the coffeehouse, which sat between a boutique that specialized in high-priced baby clothes and an empty storefront with a sign asking us to WATCH THIS SPACE FOR AN EXCITING NEW ENDEAVOR. Sam and I stopped to watch the space for a few seconds.

Nothing exciting happened at all.

The coffeehouse was packed as usual, but Eric and his little brother, Matthew, were saving us spots at one of the small tables. So much for worrying about the three-way dynamic among Sam, Eric, and me. I guess we'd just put that off for some future occasion.

Before we got in line, we swung by the table to say hi. I swear I heard Matthew humming as we approached. And I don't mean he had a song in his heart. It was more like one long, sustained buzzing sound that was far from natural for the usually shy and quiet boy.

"Not again," Sam said as we stepped up to the table.

"Again," Eric said, raising a mostly empty frozen coffee drink to the air. Optimists might say that the glass was half full, but I'm a realist. The drink was mostly empty. Considering the humming that Matthew was doing, I doubted that Eric had been the pessimist that emptied it.

"Hi, Sam!" Matthew said with another frozen drink in front of him. It had barely been touched. "Hi, Bryan. I didn't know you were coming. I haven't seen you since . . . since. . . . It's been a long time. Eric wouldn't let me come to his party or I would have seen you there. You were at the party, right? I wouldn't know because I wasn't allowed to go."

I blinked twice. "Hi," I said. Then I turned and went to get in line. Sam followed.

We weaved our way through the coffeehouse vultures waiting for a seat to open up so they could set up camp. Once we were out of earshot, I whispered to her, "That was more words than I've ever heard Matthew say. *Ever*. And I've known him since before he could even say words. He hardly even babbled much as a baby. Just sort of sat there watching the world go by and silently judging us."

"You thought a baby was judging you?"

"I think *everyone* is judging me," I said. "Besides, I was eight at the time."

"You're weird."

"I know that," I said. "But what's the kid's excuse?"

"Caffeine," Sam explained. "Does it to him every time."

I looked back at Eric and Matthew. The little guy's leg was shaking so much that the table beside them was vibrating. The faux hippie dude working on his top-of-the-line seventeen-inch MacBook Pro looked way annoyed. "Ya think maybe Eric should cut back on the caffeine?"

"He always orders his brother a noncaffeinated drink," Sam said. "Somehow Matthew always manages to switch it on Eric without him noticing."

"Maybe it's time to find another hangout," I said.

"Maybe," Sam agreed as we stepped up to the counter. "This is on me."

"Oh, you bet it is," I said. She ordered a Mocha Java, while I got a Vanilla Caramel Java and I gleefully let her pay for both. Normally, we go Dutch, but I figured that she owed me since Eric was now a part of whatever scheme she had brought me here to hatch. Besides, she sometimes gets offended when I try to pay for things or don't let her pay. That's the problem of having a friend in a totally different tax bracket.

Our drinks were ready in under a minute and we rejoined Eric and Matthew back at the table. It was still shaking along with Matthew's leg, but not as badly as before. Maybe the caffeine was working its way out of his system.

"Hey, Bryan, did you get a Vanilla Caramel? I've never had a Vanilla Caramel. Can I try it? I wanna see what it tastes like."

And maybe not.

"Matthew," Eric said, all big-brother-sternly. "I said you could come here with us if you stayed calm. So far, you've stolen my drink and annoyed half the people here with your motormouth. Keep it up and it's the last time you hang with me and my friends."

"Sorry," Matthew said, chastised. I felt bad for the kid. I'd been known to hit a good sugar buzz once in a while myself back when I was his age. Still, if I was half as annoying on sugar as Matthew was on caffeine, I would like to think someone would have sat me down and gagged me.

"Sorry," Eric said to us.

I just shrugged. There wasn't anything to really apologize for, but whatever. I had every intention of being on my best behavior. Eric had just referred to me as his "friend." It was about time I started treating him that way too, wasn't it?

There were two open seats at the table. One was a chair beside Matthew, while the other was a space on the small wicker love seat next to Eric. As much as I was trying to get used to us being "friends" again, I felt the love seating was more appropriate for him and Sam.

When Sam sat beside her beau, I couldn't help but notice how they were perfectly framed together by the wicker back of the seat. I hate to admit it, but they kind of looked cute, sitting there, sipping their drinks . . . or what Eric had left of his drink.

"Okay," Sam said, calling the meeting to order. "I think we're all worried about Hope and Drew, right?"

Eric nodded.

I shrugged. "I'm worried about *Hope*."

"You'd be worried about Drew if you knew what he did last night," Eric said. Then he finished off his drink. He didn't say anything else. I mean, come on! You don't say something like that and leave a person hanging.

"What?!" I asked.

"Okay." He looked around to make sure no one could hear him, then leaned forward. The three of us leaned in as well. "All night. Barry Manilow. On shuffle."

"Eeeeee," Sam and I said. Matthew just looked confused.

Let me explain. Drew's mom? *Total* Fanilow. She took us to a concert way back before Drew and I knew what we were getting ourselves into. The emotional scars took years to heal. If Drew was reopening old wounds, that meant things were serious all around.

"So, we agree something has to be done, right?" Sam said.

"Why?" I asked. "If they want to get back together—"

"Hope's gone at the end of next week," she reminded me. "And they can't even be in the same room. If they don't deal with it now, they might spend the summer apart and miss their chance to get back together."

The logic was flawed, but I did get what she was saying. I wasn't so sure that Hope and Drew did belong together, but, quite frankly, that wasn't my decision to make. And while some might say that it wasn't our business to interfere . . . well, as Sam kind of said earlier, that's what best friends are for.

"So, what are we going to do to get Hope and Drew back together again?" She turned to me with an expectant expression.

"And you're looking at me, why?" I asked. "This is your scheme."

"No," Sam said. "My scheme was to get you here so I could go along with your scheme. You know I suck at this."

"Sam said suck!" Matthew announced. Loudly.

I couldn't help it. I burst out laughing while Eric hung his head. Faux Hippie Dude shot us all a look then slammed his MacBook shut and huffed out of the place. Two coffeehouse vultures dove for the empty seat, nearly smashing their laptops into each other in the process.

"You tricked me," I said to Sam. "I only signed on to this thing because you said you had a scheme."

"And I refer to my previous statement," Sam said. "You *are* my scheme. So what do you want to do?"

I was flabbergasted. Actually flabbergasted. I had never been flabbergasted before. It was quite the odd feeling. Somewhere beyond shocked, but not quite dismayed.

"I don't even know where to begin," I said. "Why are you putting this on me?"

For some reason, Eric decided to chime in at that point. "I think we should—"

"Not now, babe," Sam said, gently placing her hand over Eric's. "We're not done yet." She turned back to me. "I am beseeching you. I would get on my knees if I thought they cleaned this floor with any amount of regularity. I need your manipulatively evil and brilliant mind on this."

"Okay," I said. "But I'm not quite there yet."

"You need more ego stroking?"

"No, I'm good," I said. "Just not ready to commit to an idea. In the meantime, I defer to Eric."

A brief flash of shock—or flabbergast—crossed Eric's face when I turned to him. He quickly recovered. I guess he was emboldened by my generous attempt to include him. "Why don't we re-create their first date?"

So much for that.

"I was kind of kidding about *The Parent Trap* earlier," I said to Sam.

"Uh-huh," she said, supportively squeezing her boyfriend's hand under hers. We both knew his plan was lame, but she was trying to be the good girlfriend. This? Was going to be fun to watch. "That's one possibility," she said. "Do you know what they did on their first date?"

Eric was looking at me, like I should know the answer or something.

"What?"

"Do you remember?" he asked.

"No."

"Well, it was a thought," Sam quickly said. I had a funny feeling that she knew exactly what Hope and Drew had done on their first date. Not that Sam knew Hope back then, but I'm sure it's something they've talked about. That's what girls *do*. Just as I'm equally sure that Drew never ran his date plans by Eric even though they did know one another back then. Because that's what guys *don't*.

Sam turned to me. "Got anything yet?"

"You could always force them together," I said. "Lock them in the observatory until they make up. I hear that kind of thing's worked before on people."

"I was thinking of something a little more . . ."

"Devious?"

"Subtle."

"Oh," I said. "I'm going to need some more time."

"Excuse me," Matthew said, raising his hand like he was in school. "I don't get it. *Why* are you trying to make Drew get back together with Hope?"

"Not now, Matthew," Eric said.

"It's okay," Sam said, turning to the little guy. "When two people are meant to be together, I think you should do everything in your power to help them stay together."

Matthew seemed to consider that for a moment. Then he turned to me for some reason. "Why do you think Drew and Hope belong together?"

"Hey, this one's on her," I said, lifting my Vanilla Caramel Java. "I'm just here for the coffee."

"Me too," Matthew said, staring longingly at my drink.

"Matthew!"

"What? You're all being weird. Whenever Dad tries to force me to do something, it's, like, the last thing I want to do."

I smacked my coffee down on the table. "And there it is."

"What?" Sam asked. She knew I was on to something.

"What?" Eric echoed with a look of confusion. He was still a few steps behind.

"We don't do anything to force them back together," I said, liking my scheme even more as it came out of my mouth. "You know they both expect us to try something. At least Hope does. So, we do nothing."

"Nothing?" Sam asked. "That's your big scheme?"

"No," I said. "That's not right. We do, do something. We do everything in our power to keep them apart over the next two weeks. Don't let them see each other. Don't let them talk to each other. That way, neither one of them will be able to do anything to make the other one any madder than they already are. By the time Hope's ready to leave for New York, they're going to be dying to get back together, if only to say good-bye. Then, we let nature take its course."

"I *like* it!" Sam said. Eric was nodding his head in appreciation as well.

Of course, it was possible that by keeping the two of them apart that long, Hope might actually go off to New York without seeing Drew one last time. Then they'd have the rest of the summer to get over each other. I didn't necessarily consider it a flaw in the plan.

"But we have to make sure they have time together before Hope leaves," Sam said.

Drat. Foiled again.

"There's always the observatory," I said.

"Or we could always just have a good-bye dinner for Hope and Eric," Sam suggested. "If we need an excuse."

"Well, that's a possibility too," I said. "Let's see where things go. But I still like the observatory idea."

"We'll hold that as a last resort," Sam said. I don't think she was being serious. Can't imagine why. "And thank you, Matthew," she added. "I owe you one."

"Can I come to the good-bye dinner?" he asked.

"No!" Eric said.

He continued buzzing, undaunted. "How 'bout another coffee?"

I looked down to see that my Vanilla Caramel Java was a lot emptier than I remembered it.

"Matthew!" we all yelled.

The Vagina Monologues

"Sorry we're late," Sam said with more enthusiasm than I could muster. She, Hope, and I made our way down the side aisle of Hall Hall, threw our stuff on some chairs, and hopped onstage. Everyone was standing in a lopsided circle. We slipped in between Jason and Tasha, exchanging apologetic smiles for disrupting the group's grand design.

"I always expect some stragglers in the summertime," Mr. Randall said. "Looks like one of you isn't quite awake yet."

"Almost there," I yawned, though nothing could have been further from the truth.

Phase One of our little scheme to keep Hope and Drew apart required Sam and Eric to coordinate their schedules to make sure there weren't any accidental run-ins during the week. This is why on Tuesday morning I found myself, once again, getting up before the crack of bloody dawn to begin my day.

Sam called Hope the night before suggesting that we all get together for breakfast to go over the monologues we'd chosen. Hope said she wasn't in the mood, but she eventually agreed.

I liked the idea because I couldn't pick among a few choices and I knew they could help me make my final decision. I *didn't* like the idea because it meant that I had to wake up way early, pick up Hope, and meet Sam in Santa Monica for breakfast. Which is why I was still sleepy when we got into our morning workshop. And to top it off, we were starting the day with improv.

I was in *no mood* for improv . . . or anything that required me to think.

(*Aside:* "Improv" refers to improvisational exercises. It's acting without a script. Like *Whose Line Is It Anyway?* or Nick Cannon's *Wild 'N Out.*)

"Here's the deal," Miss Julie, aka Ms. Blackstone, aka the daughter of the most famous man in modern theater, said. "We're going to start with a movement exercise. Everyone come up with an animal you want to portray. You're going to walk across the stage as that animal and we have to guess what animal you are."

Seemed simple enough. I was mentally going over my best "mooing" sound when she added, "Silently. You can't make a sound. We have to guess solely from the way you move."

Okay. A little harder, but not impossible. At least I didn't have to come up with dialogue. I was still wiping the sleep out of my eyes.

Miss Julie started us off by lumbering into the circle waving her arm in front of her from side to side. Several students yelled out "Elephant," while Jimmy Wilkey did one better by shouting, "Pachyderm!"

Me? I stood quietly as she continued walking toward Holly and tagged her to cross next. Not surprisingly, Holly chose a preening peacock to strut across the stage. This one took us slightly longer to figure out, largely because once she started wafting her hands out from her butt most of us broke into stifled hysterics.

The game continued as everyone got his or her chance. We went through snake and rabbit and chipmunk and a rather impressive impersonation of a camel with two humps. Usually, I prefer to go last in these things, but with every student chosen I lost the chance to do easier animals. We continued with giraffe and frog and an unsightly slug. (That one was Belinda, which made us all laugh.)

When Gary stepped into the circle, the entire class yelled, "Monkey!" before he even made a movement. He laughed and shook his head before moving forward with a rather convincing display of a flamingo. That boy had balance. Too bad he balanced his way over to me, making it my turn in the circle.

I guess being sleep deprived put me in a playful mood, because I went with skunk and started out by turning my fanny toward Sam and making it look like I was spraying her.

"Bryan!" she screeched, smacking my butt.

"Dog!" someone yelled out, which told me more than I wanted to know about her pet.

I crawled into the circle on all fours acting like my tail was in the air. "Bobcat!" "Coyote!" I feigned fear of predator and turned and sprayed again. "Scorpion!" Maybe I really was too tired because it was taking way longer than anyone else had. I was stuck in the circle as more and more incorrect animals were shouted out. As a last resort, I went with a Pepé Le Pew act, sure to entertain *and* get myself out of the circle.

Holly chimed in with "A sick walrus."

I shot her a look.

"A Labradoodle!" Sam burst out.

"Exactly," I lied, tapping Mr. Randall in. As I took my place back in the circle, I heard someone mumble, "I *said* dog."

Okay, that was *way* more difficult than it should have been. I continued to watch my friends and enemies as their animal choices got more and more exotic. We wound up going around the circle a few times, but thankfully, no one forced me to go again.

Once we were warmed up, we worked on voice projection. Mr. Randall and Miss Julie sat at the back of Hall Hall while the students took turns modulating the volume of our voices to make sure we could be heard. Considering how many of us were onstage, the lesson was fairly time consuming.

Finally, it came time to announce our monologue choices.

Mr. Randall had us take seats in the audience while he asked us—starting with the sophomores—which monologues we had chosen. It wasn't as easy a process as one might expect. There was a fair amount of overlap, caused by the fact that Mr. Randall had lent out his book of monologues to some of the juniors and sophomores and everyone kept picking the same pieces.

This wasn't usually a problem when we performed in class. There were only so many monologue books out there. And there were only so many parts that Orion Academy students wanted to play. (Usually, we chose wealthy yet mentally unbalanced characters. . . . I guess most of us could relate.) But with Hartley Blackstone coming to critique us and choose two students for his acting program, everyone wanted to *shine*. And that was going to be hard to do if we all performed *To be, or not to be*.

Once everything settled down, it became immediately clear that the seniors were all taking this way seriously. There was no overlap. No typical monologue choices. None of us had gone to Mr. Randall's big book of monologues for our choices.

I already knew that Sam had spent most of the night going through every monologue she could find online as well as through her own personal play collection in search of the perfect piece. She finally settled on the sarcastic and sardonic lesbian trapped in Hell, Inez from Sartre's existential classic *No Exit*. (*Aside:* The play deals with the idea that "Hell is other people." So true.) Clearly, Sam was going all out for this. In pure Sam fashion she already had the piece memorized when we'd sat down for breakfast.

Hope was doing a comic turn as Kate, the female lead from *The Taming of the Shrew*. It was a good choice. Hope was very much like the strong-willed character. It would definitely play to her strengths. At least, it would play to the strengths of the usually brash and bawdy Hope Rivera. The moody and sullen friend that was still mourning over the end of her relationship wouldn't have a chance.

Considering that Hope had chosen "sloth" as her animal choice onstage, I was beginning to worry that her mood was going to affect her performance on Friday. This was getting serious. Hope was *not* the kind of girl that let a guy get in the way of her chances at an opportunity like this.

As for me, I chose Tom from *The Glass Menagerie*. It's a drier piece than I would normally go with, but I thought it was the kind of thing Blackstone would like.

The rest of the seniors were doing a variety of pieces I knew well enough, along with a couple from plays I had only heard of in passing. Based on the selection alone, it really did seem like Jason was going to be the one to beat with his monologue from *The History Boys*.

Holly Mayflower made her followers, Alexis and Belinda, go first so she could be the last one to announce her monologue. Both Hope's stepsisters had chosen a piece from *Medea*. Considering that Alexis pronounced it like the word "media" instead of meh-DEE-a, I figure Holly had probably just handed them the monologues she wanted them to do.

When it came time for Holly to announce her monologue, I swear I heard a drumroll in the background. But maybe that was just my imagination. Or maybe she had a drummer from one of her dad's bands stationed outside the theater. The girl is known for spectacles.

She stood up in her row, took a deep breath, and announced,

"I'll be performing the part of the sensual and emotionally divided character Ivy from Jamison Montrose's groundbreaking play *The Mayflower Maxim*."

Heads all around the theater were turning to their neighbors as confused whispers filled the air. Hope and I looked right at Sam, who was a veritable walking Wikipedia of theatrical history. She just shrugged and shook her head. She'd never heard of *The Mayflower Maxim* either.

Sure, we all knew about Jamison Montrose. He was the new wunderkind on the Broadway scene and the heir apparent to Hartley Blackstone's throne. His play *Stop!* had just won the Tony for best *everything*. And he was in the pre-rehearsal for his supposedly revolutionary new musical *Go!* But even with everything about the guy in print lately, *The Mayflower Maxim* was a new one to me. And it was slightly bothersome that Holly's last name was in the title.

"*The Mayflower Maxim?*" Mr. Randall asked. "I've never heard of that play." He looked to Miss Julie, who shook her head like Sam had.

"It hasn't been produced yet," Holly said. "Jamie is . . ."

". . . a friend of Daddy's," Sam, Hope, and I whispered in unison along with Holly.

"Figures," I mumbled.

My mumbling was lost in the cacophony of voices protesting Holly's monologue. Holly was going to preview a new piece by Jamison Montrose—I'm sorry, *Jamie*—in front of Hartley Blackstone. Even if the monologue was crap, he'd probably be impressed by her connections. And really? *Ivy?* In

The Mayflower Maxim? Were we supposed to think this monologue wasn't specifically written for her: Holly *Mayflower?*
She'd brought in a ringer of a writer to write her a ringer of a
role. Combine that with her natural talent and she was even
more of a threat.

"Aren't you going to say anything?" Jason asked Sam.

"What would be the point?" Sam asked with a shrug.

Besides, everyone else was already saying enough.

"Now, hold on," Mr. Randall said, raising his hands to
implore the raging students for quiet. "Hold on. If—"

"Mr. Randall," Holly said, waving a hand. She cut him off
just as he managed to regain order. "Is there something wrong
with choosing an unproduced piece?"

"Well, it's not that, exactly," Mr. Randall said. "But—"

"No, I get it," Holly said magnanimously. Holly is very
good at magnanimous. It's *genuine* she has a problem with. "It's
just . . . this piece really spoke to me, you know? I didn't realize everyone would be so threatened by it."

Mr. Randall nodded in understanding . . . because he was
understanding what she wanted him to understand. Holly
knew she'd cause a stir when she announced that she was
doing a piece that—let's be blunt—must have been written
specifically for her. I'd be surprised if we ever heard of this
play actually opening. But Mr. Randall had always let us
choose anything we wanted for monologues we performed
in class. We were usually encouraged to seek out alternative
sources for materials, like novels, songs, and poems. I've
been hard-pressed to find any performance that matched the

emotional resonance of Tasha Valentine's dramatic reading of the list of ingredients in a Twinkie. I remember even seeing a few tears in the room by the time she had gotten to sodium stearol lactylate.

"We've always been free to do scenes or monologues from whatever sources we've found during the school year," Mr. Randall reminded us all, and let us know the direction his decision was about to go. "This program will be no different. Holly, you may use the piece."

This was met by a collection of groans.

Holly was on top of that too. "No, Mr. Randall. I'll be fine. I'm sure I can pick something else out. And don't worry at all about it cutting into my rehearsal time. I don't need as much prep time as other people."

"Oh, for crying out loud," Sam said softly. Then, she added loudly, "Holly, do the damn piece. You know you're going to, anyway."

Holly regarded our group with practiced innocence.

"Why, thank you, Sam," Holly said. "I never expected you to be on my side."

"Oh, I'm *full* of surprises," Sam replied with a smile.

"I can't wait for you to see it," Holly said.

Sam's smile was still frozen tightly in place. "Neither can I."

Noises Off

We broke for lunch after Mr. Randall finished recording our monologue selections. Not surprisingly, no two people would be reciting the same monologue, although Alexis and Belinda would be performing the same character. And I couldn't *wait* to see that.

In spite of—or maybe because of—the fact that their mom is a bitter, washed-up actress, neither of Hope's steps had ever set foot on a stage before. The two of them preferred to spend their life in the audience, commenting on the action rather than taking part in it. Can't say I blame them. It's easier to talk about people than to be talked about by people.

Figuring we could get in some extra rehearsals—and keep Hope away from Drew—Sam arranged for us to lunch in her mom's classroom. Anne's room was locked during the summer, but she gave her daughter the key. Hope stayed behind to talk to Mr. Randall for a minute as Sam, Jason, and I split off from the maddening crowd and wound our way through the empty halls.

"It's cool that your mom will let us use her room," Jason said. I tend to forget how convenient it is to have a parent (or pseudo-parent since she's not *my* mom) on staff. "We can really use this time to get in some good work."

Sam shrugged, blushing. "It balances out how annoying it can be for my mom to be around all the time." I always find it funny when Sam acts like she's annoyed that Anne works at the same school she goes to. They're like the closest mother-daughter act this side of Mama Rose and Gypsy . . . okay, bad example.

Once inside the empty room, the three of us pulled chairs up to Anne's desk and brought out our lunches. While we ate, Jason took a *one-hundred pound* Shakespeare anthology out of his bag and slammed it down on the desk.

"I hope you don't mind," Jason said as he heaved the book open, "but I kind of found a scene for us last night."

Sam and I looked at each other. Jason was certainly *eager*. That was not really a surprise. But I think we both were a little wary that he was jumping so far ahead with our scene. We hadn't even started working on our monologues yet.

"What scene?" Sam asked tentatively.

"I read through *Twelfth Night*. There's a problem with the play. Different characters keep running in and out of all the scenes, so it's hard to find a good four-person scene. I tried to cut together a few scenes but no matter what I tried, the best I could come up with would leave at least one of us with about a line and a half. I hope you don't mind, but I thought maybe we should do a different play."

I looked at Sam, waiting for a reaction. All she did was nod at him to go on. We usually had some of our best debates over what scenes we would do for class. Even when we both agreed on a piece, it was far more interesting to argue the merits to make sure we were choosing the right one. I know. We're weird. But sometimes a good battle of wits can be fun if you've got a similarly armed opponent. We'd never really worked on scenes with Jason before. I'm guessing she didn't want to scare him off by being too opinionated.

"I flipped through *A Midsummer Night's Dream* and found a really great scene with the four main characters that should be fun to do. I made copies." He handed us some pages he had stuck in the back of his book.

"Wait a minute," I said. "You went through two Shakespeare plays *and* picked your monologue last night?"

"I was excited," he explained. "I couldn't sleep."

When I can't sleep, I lie in the dark staring at the ceiling. Jason? Studies Shakespeare texts.

"I know this scene," Sam said after a quick perusal. "It's kind of an obvious choice, but it shows some range. I'm in."

I barely glanced at the pages. "Then I guess I'm in too." If both Sam and Jason liked it, I doubted that I'd find anything wrong with the scene. It was *Shakespeare*, after all. Since Sam wasn't up for a debate, I figured I wasn't going to start one. It would be inappropriate to fight in front of Jason. Actually, I was just afraid to lose. He clearly knew his Shakespeare, whereas I knew how to count the cracks in my ceiling with only the moonlight to see by.

We all have our talents.

Before we finalized the decision, Sam remembered that we weren't a trio. "We'll just have to see what Hope—"

"CAN I *HELP* YOU WITH SOMETHING?" Hope's voice boomed from the hallway, causing us to jump out of our chairs. Aside from the shock of the unexpected yell, it was also a surprise to hear Hope raise her voice, considering her mood of late.

The three of us looked up to the doorway to see Alexis and Belinda breathing heavily with their hands pressed to their hearts . . . or the spaces their hearts would have been had they actually had hearts. Figures, the one thing that would bring her out of her silence would be the steps.

"Scare us to death, why don't you!" Alexis shot back.

"Maybe next time," Hope threatened. "If I catch you eavesdropping on my group again."

"We were just coming to talk to you," Belinda said. "To see if you needed a ride home later."

"And you couldn't wait until after lunch?" Hope asked. "We're not leaving for another three hours."

"We were just trying to be helpful," Belinda said.

"Yeah. Last time we do that," Alexis added as she grabbed her twin by the arm and stormed off.

Hope watched them leave before coming into the room and making a point of shutting the door behind her.

"What was that about?" Jason asked.

"They probably wanted to find out what we were doing so they could report back to Holly," Hope said.

We nodded. I wanted to say something about Hope raising her voice, but I didn't know how to do it without sounding stupid. I think Sam was having the same internal debate because we both kind of stood there with confused looks on both our faces.

"So, what *were* we doing?" Hope finally asked. Her tone was softer than usual, but it was nice to see her interested in something.

"Picking a scene for next week," Sam replied. I could hear the concern in her voice. If Holly knew what scene we planned to perform, she'd choose a scene specifically with the intention of showing our team up. Not that she'd have much of a chance of showing us up with Alexis and Belinda in her group, but she could try.

"Should we pick a new scene?" I asked.

"No," Sam said with absolute certainty. "I'm not about to fall into Holly's trap. We shouldn't make our choice based on what she may or may not do to sabotage us."

"Good," Hope said softly, but firmly.

"I'm with you guys," I added. "But, then again, I'm always with you."

Jason nodded his head. We were united in our selection. Or, technically, we were united against Holly. Either way, we had a scene, so we could get down to work on other things. Our monologue performances were only a few days away.

"What did we choose?" Hope asked as she joined us with her lunch. Jason and Sam filled her in on the scene while I munched on my food. It was interesting listening to them both talk Shakespeare. So much more fun than listening to Sam discuss soccer with her boyfriend.

"No more talk of scenes," Sam decreed once they got that business out of the way. "We need to focus on monologues."

"Speaking of which," I said, turning to Hope. "What did you talk to Mr. Randall about?"

"I've changed my monologue choice," she replied.

"But *Taming of the Shrew* is perfect for you," Sam said.

Death Glare! Death Glare!

"No . . . I mean . . ." There was no way Sam was going to get out of this one unscathed.

"Why did you change it?" I asked, deflecting Hope's anger. As scary as it was, it was nice to see it again. Maybe Sam and I had overreacted about Hope's mood. It could have just been normal end-of-relationship stuff she was dealing with.

"When Mr. Randall said we could do unproduced work, it got me thinking. I'm going to write myself a monologue."

"Really?" Sam and I asked in unison. This was not a good idea.

"Might as well put my mood to work for me," Hope said.

Oh no. Oh, no no no.

Don't get me wrong. Hope is an amazing writer. I had no doubt that she could create the monologue to end all monologues. What worried me—and Sam too, I'm sure—was the whole "putting her mood to work" for her part. At that moment, her mood was definitely reflected in her eyes. She had chosen the black contacts that were all pupil and no iris. Those blank eyes always freaked me out. And I was *really* afraid of what those eyes could come up with in terms of a monologue. I could easily see her putting everything she felt into her speech. That level of honesty and openness could really backfire on her, considering that we go to a school where gossip is a weapon and truth is ammunition.

Without a word, Sam and I silently agreed that it was even more important to keep Hope away from Drew that week. The last thing Hope needed was to add any fuel to that fire.

We spent the rest of the lunch hour working in silence while we individually broke down our monologues into beats. (*Aside:* That's something you do so you know where to take the proper moments. Examine the motivation for each and every line. Know when to take an action. That kind of thing.) Well, three of us were working on our monologue break-downs. Hope was writing her own monologue on the back of her copied pages from *The Taming of the Shrew.* From what I could tell, she wasn't getting much actual writing down, but a lot of crossing things out and starting over.

Every time she scratched something else out I got a deeper feeling of impending doom.

With five minutes left in lunch, Sam put down her pencil and announced: "Okay, everyone, papers to the front of the room." She handed me her monologue. Jason looked confused, but he did the same.

"This is what Bryan does," Sam explained to Jason as I went to work on her monologue. "He's, like, an expert at scene breakdowns. Trust me. You won't be disappointed."

I felt my face going red. It was true, if I do say so myself. I had this crazy natural talent for breaking down a monologue. It was the actual presenting it onstage that I always had a problem with.

You know. The important part.

Once I was done, I handed Sam's back for her to look at and went over Jason's with him. "I think if you keep these lines together and build on the moment here"—I pointed out the passage I was talking about—"you'll have a much stronger moment. You know. If you want to. It works the other way too."

"No," Jason said. "Thanks. This is much better."

I was blushing again. I could feel it.

"Good job," Sam said, putting her own monologue back in her bag without questioning any of my suggestions. She checked her watch. "Lunch is almost over."

We all got up and left the room, making sure that Sam locked up behind us.

"I need to swing by my locker," Hope said.

"We'll go too," Sam said. "Meet you back at the auditorium, Jason."

"Okay," he said, and went off in the other direction.

"My locker's on the other side of school," Hope reminded us. "We're going to be late. You don't have to come with me."

"No prob," Sam said, grabbing Hope by the arm and pulling her along. "We'll be late together, 'cause *it's friendship . . . friendship . . . just the perfect blends*—"

A locker door slamming echoed through the hall.

"Let's cut through the courtyard," Sam said as she kicked open the outer door that led outside. "It's faster that way."

"No, it's no—" Sam grabbed me by the collar and pulled me out after them. As I crossed over the threshold, I looked back to see Eric standing by his locker and guiding Drew off the other way.

Oh.

The Forced Marriage

The brief spark of life that Hope had shown during lunch Tuesday was pretty much gone by the time we got back to the auditorium. And as the next couple days passed, I wasn't so sure that our scheme was helping out all that much either.

Keeping Hope and Drew apart didn't seem to be having an effect on either of them. Hope remained sullen and quiet. She spent all of her time working on her monologue in a new journal she had purchased solely for that purpose. Either she had a lot to get off her ample chest or she had decided to turn her monologue into a one-woman show. I wouldn't know, since she still refused to show us what she was doing or talk about her feelings with Sam.

Drew didn't seem to be doing any better. The one time I passed him in the hallway, I swear I heard the pulsing beat of the *Copacabana* coming from the headphones he had on.

Our scheme wasn't even all that much of a challenge either. Hope went where we told her to go and she did what we told her to do. If Sam turned us down a hall we didn't need to go down, Hope followed without question. When I drove Electra at two miles an hour to school to make sure we'd be late, Hope didn't even slam her foot down on the gas pedal to make us go faster. Not that she would have done that normally, but she would have at least questioned why an elderly man with a walker was passing us on his daily stroll. It was like the only motivation she felt was for writing in her journal. I was beginning to worry about her monologue performance. Not just what she was going to say, but if she was going to be able to say anything at all.

But her monologue wasn't the only one I was concerned about. My prep was not evolving the way I wanted either. Then again, I don't know of any actor who is ever happy with his work, so maybe I was doing better than I thought.

For the rest of the week, our classwork had been focused on vocal exercises, projection, and stage presence. Anything that would help us give a better performance on Friday. The actual rehearsal of our monologues had been left for outside of school on our own. My group didn't even work on them in Anne's classroom over lunch. We all felt that it was better to do the preliminary rehearsing by ourselves so that we didn't interfere with one another's choices. Of course, we had no intention of going onstage Friday without getting other opinions.

It's a long-standing tradition in our trio that Sam, Hope, and I always preview our work together the night before any performance. Since Jason was part of our scene group, we invited him to join us. We chose to do it at my house because it was the most convenient for us. The location also helped us with a new phase of our plan to see if Hope and Drew were meant to be back together.

Sam went first, as she usually did. She'd also go last. She would go in every position if we let her. Sam likes to work a scene to death. She's not happy with a piece until the moment of her performance, and even then she wants to go back and do some things over to prove to herself that she did everything she could in the first place. I've tried to explain to her that there is such a thing as over-rehearsing, but she refuses to believe me.

Sam was amazing, as usual. Inez was a very different character for her. Usually, Sam plays the innocent ingenue. Like Dorothy in *The Wizard of Oz*. *No Exit* was a bit of a darker choice than she normally made. Inez was about as strong-willed as a pre-breakup Hope. But Sam really worked the part. She had us all shouting, "Brava!" by the end. (*Aside: Brava* is the feminine form of *bravo*. Yes, even applause can be sexist.)

"Comments? Questions?" Sam asked after a bow.

Neither Jason nor Hope had anything to say. I, however, did have a question. "Why did you start out with so much intensity?"

"This is the part where Inez finally blows up," Sam said. "I wanted to come in big."

"Yeah," I said. "But then you kept building from that moment. You might want to try opening big, then taking it down a bit and building up to the end. I think you had too many big moments. It might be better to tone some of it down. But still . . . amazing performance."

"Thanks," Sam said as she dropped beside me on the couch.

Jason went next. His performance was almost as good as Sam's. I wasn't familiar with *The History Boys*, or Jason's character, but I got what he was saying and understood the moments he was playing like I knew the play by heart. The only weakness I could see was that he swallowed some of his lines. Sam and Hope also caught that one. We all suggested that he play things out to the audience a bit more and then moved on to me.

I wish I could tell you that my performance was so good that my friends couldn't even come up with a note to give me. But, that was *far* from the truth.

"You need to ground your character in reality a bit more," Jason suggestion.

"Really?" Hope asked. "I thought he should play up the dream element. It's like he's recalling a memory, not simply narrating a play."

I looked to Sam, who was the one person I trusted most when it came to acting advice. "I think they're both right," Sam said. "You're playing the lines, not the emotion." I nodded. I got what she was saying, but I wasn't so clear on how I could translate it into my acting.

They had some more specific comments for me that I listened to diligently while I wondered how I was going to incorporate it all into my performance by the next morning. Just as I reached the point of total saturation, Sam suggested we move on to Hope.

"We can't wait to see this magnum opus of yours," I said, glad to have the focus off me. I was trying to keep the moment light, but I could tell that Sam was just as concerned as I was over what we were about to see. Hope had been keeping us in the dark on her monologue since she announced she was writing one herself. She wouldn't even tell us what the subject was, but we had our guesses. And they were all the same guess. Now that we were finally going to see it, we were on the edge of the couch in anticipation.

We all—including Jason—braced for impact.

"Um," Hope said. "It's not quite ready yet."

Sam shook her head. "Uh-uh. We always share our work the night before a scene. No backing out. That's the rule. Now go."

It wasn't that either of us were hurt that Hope didn't want to perform her piece in front of us—well, maybe a little—but Sam and I were mostly concerned. With the wounds of her breakup still fresh, we were worried Hope would get up onstage in front of everyone—most notably her steps—and pour out her heart. And *that* would not be good for anyone. Well, the steps would probably think it was hilarious, but the rest of us would be feeling varying degrees of discomfort and pity for her. And neither Sam nor I wanted any of that.

Then again, maybe Hope was writing a lovely piece about the beauty of summertime and the excitement of a future laid out before her.

Riiight.

"No," Hope said. Her voice was calm, but her tone was

firm. "I want my performance to be fresh. I'm not rehearsing it at all. When I set foot onstage, I want the words to come out of me naturally. With genuine emotion."

Now I was really worried about this monologue. And Hope in general.

"Hope, you have to rehearse," I said. "You have to find a character. Block your movements. Otherwise you're just reading a diary entry, which . . . *interesting*, but not acting."

Sam and I spent the next few minutes trying to convince Hope to at least show us what she was working on, but she wouldn't budge. The scary part was that she didn't even argue with us. She just shut down and let us do all the talking, which is *so* not like Hope. I gave up when I realized we weren't getting anywhere, but Sam had one more point to make.

"You'll never get into Blackstone's program if he thinks you're just going up there and being yourself," she said.

This, at least, got a response. "Sam, there are more important things in this world than Hartley Blackstone's acting program," Hope said. I thought Sam was about to fall over on that one. "But don't worry. I do intend to play a role . . . a role unlike any other I've ever played before."

Duhn-duhn-duhn!

As if on cue, there was a knock at the kitchen door. Actually, it wasn't entirely on cue as it came several minutes earlier than it should have. Sam and I shared a knowing glance that we hoped Hope didn't catch and then excused ourselves to check on who we thought was our not-so-mystery guest. Turns out it wasn't who we were expecting. It was my not-somysterious mom and her best friend and business partner, Blaine.

"Thanks Bryan, I couldn't reach my key," Mom said as she came through the door loaded down by a box of doggie-related merchandise. This was almost routine around the house lately. She'd been bringing a lot of stuff home from her store so she could work on the designs in her studio. Kaye 9 may be one of the more popular stores on Melrose Avenue, but all the magic happens in a small work space that was once our garage.

I grabbed the box from her and put it down on the kitchen table, taking a peek inside to see what she brought home to work on. It appeared to be her fall line, as there was an abundance of browns and oranges in the mix. This is what I hate about retail. Summer hadn't even begun for me yet, and Mom was already focused on back to school. She even had little doggie backpacks in there . . . for their little doggie textbooks?

"Hey, kiddo," Blaine said as he came in carrying two more boxes. Even with his arms loaded down, he still managed to flip back my fedora and muss my hair. "Hi, Samilina."

"Hey, Blainerosa," Sam said.

Don't ask me. They came up with those nicknames entirely on their own.

Blaine . . . or *Blainerosa* . . . is the brains behind Kaye 9, while Mom is the heart, soul, and creative vision. That's not to say that I don't think my mom is smart. She's incredibly gifted when it comes to art and design and she may even have a little dog whisperer in her. But Blaine's the one with the business savvy. If it weren't for him, Mom would probably be stuck in a mall kiosk somewhere.

Before the kitchen door could close behind them, the headmaster's dog came bounding inside.

"Get the gate! The gate!" Mom yelled.

Sam lunged for the doggie gate that we kept in the space beside the refrigerator and the doorway, but she couldn't move fast enough. Canoodle burst out of the kitchen and into the rest of the house, leaving a trail of paw prints on the beige carpet.

"Canoodle!" Mom yelled as she gave chase.

Another dog poked her head in through the back door before it closed. Mal kind of looked in like she was asking if the coast was clear before she plodded into the room and right up to me. Mal is Blaine's Labrador, and the closest thing I have to a cousin in this or any other world. She seemed thrilled to see me, even as she glanced toward the still ungated doorway to the rest of the house. To this day, Mal (which is short for Maleficent) has never been past that threshold. Rather than appearing jealous that Canoodle had gotten to the promised land and making her own attempt at freedom, Mal just shook her head as if she had already had enough of that crazy dog.

I could relate.

Jason heard the commotion and wrangled Canoodle back into the kitchen. Once the dust had settled, further greetings were exchanged and we decided to take a snack break. As we gathered around the center island for our milk and cookies, *that* was when the not-so-mystery guest arrived.

"Hello?" Eric called out with a tentative knock on the kitchen door that sent Canoodle into hysterics. Mal looked up at me like she was embarrassed for the entire canine race.

Since Blaine was the closest to the door, he got it.

"Mr. Blaine!" Eric said in surprise.

"Please . . . just Blaine," he replied. "Mr. Blaine makes me sound like a gay hairdresser . . . and I am *not* a hairdresser."

Blaine is a man of many nicknames, but nothing about him would ever be mistaken for the stereotypical hairdresser often portrayed in Hollywood. He struck an imposing figure in the doorway, all two-hundred-fifty pounds of muscle on him. His hand swallowed Eric's as they shook. Back when we were kids, my friends used to call Blaine "Mr. Blaine." (Kind of like Miss Julie, I guess.) I always liked it, because I was the only one that got to drop the "Mr." when I called him by name. There was a time when I called him "Uncle Blaine," but that got cumbersome quick, so it's pretty much always been Blaine for me.

If my calculations are right, Eric hadn't seen Blaine since my grandfather's funeral, back when we were fourteen.

"Eric Whitman," Blaine said. "Where have you been keeping yourself?"

"I've been around," Eric said.

"He's here for Sam," I clarified, realizing I just blew our cover in front of Hope. This was supposed to look like a spontaneous visit. "I mean . . . I assume he's here for Sam. Unless you need me for something?"

"Smooth," Sam whispered as she pushed past me to give her boyfriend a kiss hello. "I told him I'd be here rehearsing."

"I got that thing for you," he said as he handed a bag to her. I guess he was as bad at the subterfuge as I was. How hard was it to come up with a noun to describe the "thing" in the bag? Especially considering there was obviously something *in* the bag and that something *did* have an actual name.

"Thanks," Sam said as she put the bag down on the table without opening it. Would it have killed her to at least *act* like she was surprised over the gift? Maybe take a peek inside? We were really blowing this one.

Thankfully, Jason helped us along without even knowing he was giving us some much needed assistance. "Hey," he said, "you want to stay and watch us run through our monologues again?"

Considering how poorly Sam and I were doing with our little charade, I fully expected Eric to stumble all over himself. Jason had jumped in and moved up our script. Sam was supposed to ask Eric to stay after we used some other stalling tactics first. But Sam's boyfriend covered like a pro. "I really shouldn't," Eric said, trying to sound nonchalant about his next line. "I left Drew in the car."

Sam, Eric, and I watched Hope perform a not-so-subtle glance out the kitchen door. There was a kind of wistfulness to the look that led me to believe that she was starting to miss Drew a bit.

"He didn't want to come in?" Hope asked.

"I told him to wait," Eric explained, following our script. "I figured you two didn't want to see each other."

"It would have been okay," Hope said with another dash of wistful thrown in.

"Next time I'll know," Eric said. Then he did something every actor dreads. He looked right at me because he knew I had the next line. He was supposed to wait for me to start speaking before he looked at me. Now, it seemed like he was waiting for me to say something.

I had to speak quickly to cover it. "You have to at least stay to see Sam's monologue."

Eric pulled up a stool. "I guess a minute wouldn't hurt. That is, if Sam doesn't mind doing it in front of all of us."

Sam? Mind having an audience? Not likely.

"I still have some things to work out," Sam said. "But . . . okay."

The rest of us got comfortable around the kitchen while Sam went through her preparations. Girl can't read so much as the title of a play without going through some warm-up exercises. Usually, it was pretty annoying, but this time I knew she was warming up with a purpose, so I didn't mind as much.

While she went through her vocal routine the three of us schemers watched as Hope watched the door. Apparently, we weren't the only ones watching.

Blaine made a move for the kitchen door. "I'll get Drew," he said. "He might want to see this too."

"That's okay," Sam, Eric, and I said *way* too earnestly . . . and too much in unison.

The room went silent for a moment. Sam hadn't even covered with vocal exercises. Everyone was waiting for one of us to explain why we didn't want Drew in the house.

Thankfully, Eric came through with an excuse. "He's on his cell phone," he explained.

"Besides, I'm ready to go," Sam said as she launched into her monologue. This time, it was even better than her first performance. Sam really feeds off an audience. I couldn't wait until the following day when she'd have all the Drama Geeks there along with Mr. Randall, Miss Julie, and most important, Hartley Blackstone himself.

As she finished, we rewarded her with heartfelt applause. Sam had taken my suggestion about varying her levels and it really added to the performance, if I do say so myself. While we were still clapping, Drew slipped inside, without bothering to knock, just like when we were kids.

Mom was the first to see him. "Drew! Honey, it's been ages. How's your family?"

"Fine, thanks," Drew said, trying—and failing—to keep his eyes off Hope.

"We should get back to work," I suggested.

"Work!" Mom exclaimed, scaring us all. "I almost forgot. I need to get that . . . thing from my studio."

"The materials order forms," Blaine reminded her.

"I know," she said. Blaine and I didn't believe her for a second. Mom could be kind of scattered at times. For instance, she was an incredibly polished and well-dressed woman. But somehow she always seemed to be missing a button. On her shirt. On her skirt. Wherever. The outfit she was currently wearing had *two* buttons missing, which usually signified that she was under some stress. Mom pushed past me and stepped over the doggie gate to head to her studio.

"Thanks for this, Eric," Sam said with a nod to the mystery

bag as she walked him to the door. Again, would it have hurt for her to give "this" a name?

"No problem," Eric said, with a kiss. "Coming, Drew?"

"Yeah," Drew said with a last glance at Hope. "Bye."

"Bye," Hope said.

"Bye!" I said a little cheerily.

Eric and Drew left without a backward glance.

"Back to work," I repeated, waving our little acting troupe in the direction of the living room. Jason led the way, but as we filed out of the kitchen, I felt a massive hand come down on top of my fedora, squishing it to my head. I decided to hang back a moment to see what Blaine wanted. It seemed the smart thing to do.

Once my friends were gone, Blaine looked me right in the eye and said, "Care to tell me what that was about?"

"What?" I asked oh-so-innocently. "We're rehearsing."

"That thing with Drew and Hope," Blaine said, crossing his arms and looking at me with a challenging eye that neither of my parents could even come close to pulling off.

Busted!

The Tragical History
of Dr. Faustus

My mind was working on a half dozen different excuses that didn't sound remotely believable, even to me. There was no way I was going to be able to fool Blaine. I couldn't manage that on my best day. And, as my little display a few minutes earlier had proven, this was *far* from my best day . . . at least where scheming and deception were concerned. So, I spilled. Everything from the breakup, to Sam's and my scheme, to our earlier performance that had been meant to tease Hope and Drew without actually letting them spend time together.

When I was done, I waited in silence for Blaine to tell me what an idiot I was for going along with the plan.

This time, however, he surprised me by not prefacing his commentary with an insult and got right to the heart of the matter. "Do Hope and Drew even want to get back together?"

"Neither one of them will talk about it," I said. "But they seem miserable now that they're apart."

"Yeah," Blaine said. "That's called a breakup. They're supposed to be miserable. If they were happy, they'd be together."

"What if they're miserable *because* they're not together?"

"Better question," Blaine said. "Do *you* think they're better off as a couple?"

I wondered what *my* opinion had to do with any of this. Blaine's question had to go unanswered because the doorbell rang, providing the distraction I was looking for. "Who could that be?" I asked. "All my friends are here."

"One way to find out," Blaine said, giving me a gentle shove in the direction of the front door.

"I got it," I yelled to no one. Mom couldn't hear the doorbell from her studio. It was soundproof. She designed it that way so she wouldn't be distracted while working on her latest doggie creations. She takes her work very seriously.

"It's like Grand Central Station in here," Sam commented as I passed by the living room. When I opened the door to find Holly, Alexis, and Belinda standing on my steps, I wished that it *were* Grand Central and that I was on the next train out of town. I had no clue what the three witches would be doing on my doorstep, and I really didn't care to find out.

"Yes?" I asked, without bothering to hide my surprise. Dropping in unexpected was not the Holly Mayflower style. She usually called ahead to give one time to roll out the red carpet and lay rose petals along the walk.

"We need to see Hope," Alexis said, rather bluntly if you ask me.

"Um . . . Hope!" I called back to the living room. "Your sisters are here."

"*Step*sisters!" she yelled back.

I smiled at the girls in the doorway, waiting for Hope to come out. Or to say something more. Or to respond in some way, shape, or form.

But . . . nothing.

"HOPE!" I called out again.

"Why don't you show the young ladies into the house?" Blaine asked from behind me. For such a large man, he moved with quite the stealth. I hadn't known that I was followed from the kitchen.

"Please, come into the house, young ladies," I said as I stepped aside.

As they walked in, I could see Holly shoot a look at the twins, rolling her eyes at our modest furnishings. When I say "modest," I mean by Malibu standards. Considering that our house is only a one-floor, three-bedroom ranch style and we don't have any Picassos in the foyer, Holly probably equated my family's housing situation with that of the characters in *Rent*.

Not that Blaine caught the look, mind you. It was only meant for me.

I didn't bother to introduce Blaine as etiquette might demand. As far as I could remember, he never would have met Holly before. Maybe the twigs, but I wasn't sure. Either way, I didn't think it would be important for him to know who they were, and I was fine not bothering to explain it. I guess he caught on to what I was up to since he didn't introduce himself either. He did watch me the entire time with an expression that suggested I was committing a major faux pas.

Pinocchio gets a tiny cricket as his conscience. Me? I warrant a two-hundred-fifty-pound bald black man.

I showed the girls into the living room where all rehearsing had stopped and posturing had begun. When I had breezed past the room to get the door, Sam and Hope had both been lounging on the couch while Jason prepped to do his monologue. Now, the girls were both standing with their arms folded in front of them. They were prepared for war. Poor Jason looked confused. Like he was aware of the tension, but not sure why it was there.

"What are you doing here?" Hope asked with more venom in her voice than the situation demanded. It was odd, considering her general malaise of the past few days, but strangely good to hear. The old Hope was back. At least, for the moment.

"We need the car," Alexis said, getting right to the point.

"I have it tonight," Hope said. "That was the arrangement. I get Thursdays so you two can have the weekend."

"I know it's a lot to ask," Belinda said, "but if you could get someone to drive you home, we could really use it."

Hope looked over the nicer of the two twigs. Belinda is the real one to watch out for. She's all sugar while her twin is the spice. Belinda has a way of forcing you to give in to what she wants simply because you'd seem like an ass saying no to her.

Not that Hope cared about that. "No."

"We need it to get ready for Mom's party," Alexis said.

"Party?" I asked. That? Was a mistake.

"You didn't know?" Holly slipped in the question in a tone suggesting that I was clearly an idiot for being unaware of the social event of the season.

"None of us are going," Hope said.

Belinda looked genuinely shocked. "I thought your dad—"

"Yes. He talked to me," Hope said. "And I told him I'm not going. Now, if you don't mind, we are trying to work here."

"We still need the car," Alexis said.

"And you're still not getting it," Hope replied. I couldn't believe that Hope was actually fighting over the pink-and-purple Mini-monstrosity. Then again, I didn't think this argument was over a car at all.

"Fine," Holly said, plopping herself down on my couch. Funny. I didn't remember inviting her to stay. When you're Holly Mayflower, I guess formal invitations don't matter much. "Since we have to cancel our plans, we might as well hang here. I'm sure you guys could use some help with your monologues."

"Ha!" Sam laughed. "Not a chance."

Holly looked over her competition. "Not ready to show anyone yet? I understand. Some people need to polish right up to the last second. While others . . ." She let her sentence hang.

"While others," Sam said, "have trouble realizing just how much work they still need."

Now, normally, I'm the least confrontational in the bunch and would have stopped this before Holly even wormed her way into the house. But I was having too much fun watching

Sam go toe-to-toe with Holly. I was also waiting to see how long it took for Hope to lay a smackdown on her steps. I guess Jason felt the need to rush in and be the gentleman, though.

"I'll be going home soon," he said. "I like to get a full eight hours' sleep before a performance. Hope, I can take you home if you want." Damn Jason and his theater rituals. We were spoiling for a good fight. Then again, that was still a possibility. Hope looked like she was about to kill him for giving her steps the opportunity to take the car.

"The car is mine on Thursday nights," Hope repeated. "That was the deal." At this point, even I was getting uncomfortable. I'm all for standing your ground, but she didn't live that far from me. Any one of us could have driven her home.

Alexis pulled out her cell phone and hit the speed dial. "If you want to play it that way." Once the phone connected, Alexis said, "Mom. She won't budge." There was a brief pause, then she handed the phone to Hope.

Knowing better than to let the phone hang in the air, Hope put it to her ear. She didn't say anything, but we could all hear her stepmom's voice on the other end. We couldn't make out what she was saying, but it was certainly shrill.

Hope didn't say a word, but we could all hear her teeth grinding. The noise was even scaring the dogs. In the kitchen!

Eventually, the voice on the other end died out and Hope flipped the cell phone shut, probably wishing she could do the same thing to her stepmom. "Fine," she said, reaching into her purse. She pulled out the car keys and threw them at Alexis. Belinda managed to snatch them out of the air in an impressive move that saved her sister from a big red welt on her cheek.

Pity.

"Looks like somebody got up on the wrong side of the breakup this morning," Holly said as she stood. "This is why relationships are overrated. They never end well. Or they don't end at all, which is just as bad."

"Sounds like justification for someone who's never had a long-term boyfriend," Sam said.

"Oh, I've had plenty of long-term boyfriends," Holly said. "Just, none of them were mine."

I showed them to the door, but Holly wasn't done yet.

"By the way," she said to Sam, "where *is* your boyfriend tonight?"

I intervened before things got ugly. "He was here earlier," I said, opening the door.

"Hmm," Holly replied. "Wonder where he is now?"

"Probably with Drew someplace fun," Alexis added.

"Maybe we can catch up with them," Belinda threw in for good measure.

Holly and the twigs left on that final note. I think Hope and Sam were about to fight over who got to slam the door behind them. In the end, Blaine took hold of it and closed it gently. I was too busy formulating a new plan.

"So," I said, trying to break the remaining tension. "What's this party their mom is throwing?" Notice how I didn't refer to the woman as Hope's stepmom. We tried to refrain from any acknowledgement that there was a relationship between Hope and the woman.

"DVD release party," Hope said. "It's the twenty-fifth anniversary of *On Angel's Wings*."

"*On Angel's Wings!*" Blaine screeched uncharacteristically from his spot hovering in the background. "I *love* that movie!" Then, he hit us with the familiar quote that was—I kid you not—etched into the glass door on the front of Hope's home. *"One voice is enough to beat back the devil when it's the voice of an angel."*

What can I say? It's a big door.

"Yeah," I said. "Hope's dad is married to Kara Bow." That's a stage name, by the way. We don't know her real name and don't really care to find out.

"How did I not know that?" Blaine asked with an accusatory glare in my direction.

"It's not that big a deal," Hope said, uncomfortably. She hated talking about her stepmom's past success . . . emphasis on *past*.

On Angel's Wings was this movie musical that Hope's stepmom starred in when she was a teen. It's the story of a fallen angel named Sylvia Angel (seriously) who needs to find her way back to Heaven through the power of song. All the while, the devil tries to keep her on Earth by posing as a recording artist and pretending to fall in love with her. It's kind of a rip-off of *Xanadu* but without the credibility of having Olivia Newton-John and Gene Kelly in the cast. (*Aside*: If you've never seen *Xanadu*, put this book down right now and go rent it. The movie is cheese-tastic!)

"So, when's the party?" Blaine asked.

"Tomorrow night," Hope said. "And that's exactly why I didn't want to give Alexis and Belinda the car. Everything for the party is already done. Kara hired a team of party planners. The steps just wanted the car so they could go clubbing on Sunset with Holly. Last time they went together, Holly hooked up with some random guy and forced Alexis and Belinda to take a cab home!" She ended her rant by calmly telling Blaine, "I can put you on the guest list for the party . . . if you want."

I've never seen Blaine so excited, yet at the same time, he managed to maintain his composure and not *look* like he was totally excited. Just another reason why he is the coolest adult I know. "If it wouldn't be too much to ask," he simply said.

"No problem at all," Hope said as she grabbed her bag. "You can go in my place." We said our good-byes, and Hope and Jason left in his car. Sam, who had borrowed her mom's car, was still hanging around.

"Your mother's been gone a long time," Blaine said once everyone was gone. "I'd better go check on her."

"Yeah," I agreed. "She probably forgot what she was look-ing for."

Blaine nodded ruefully and left the room.

As soon as he was gone, I hopped on the couch beside Sam and announced, "New scheme!"

"I'm tingling with anticipation."

"We've been doing this all wrong," I said. "We don't need Hope to be miserable. We need her to be mad. That's when Hope gets all decisive."

"True."

"And who can bring her from zero to insane in point-five seconds?"

"Alexis and Belinda."

"Exactly," I said. "So how insane do you think Hope would be if one of her steps was moving in on Drew?"

"In. Sane. But isn't that like making some kind of deal with the devil?"

"Like you said about Hope earlier. We don't have to *tell* the girls what we're doing. All we need to do is set up the situation. I have complete faith in Alexis and Belinda to be able to take it from there."

"And what if it backfires and Drew does hook up with one of them? Or *both* of them?"

"Okay. Didn't need *that* picture, thank you."

"I didn't mean at the same time! Eww!"

I shook the image from my brain. "Drew can't stand either of them. Never could. So we don't have to worry about it. Then again, that would prove one way or another whether or not his relationship with Hope is truly over."

Sam considered what I was saying. "Remind me never to make you angry."

"You know I only use my powers for good," I said.

"Yeah, but whose definition of 'good' are you going with?"

"Point taken."

The Crucible

Sam and I put our scheme on hold Friday morning because we didn't need anything to distract us from the auditions. I was nervous enough. I didn't need to be working on ways to manipulate people. Besides, we were too busy on the ride in trying to get Hope to show us her monologue to worry about anything else.

"No," Hope said for the tenth time as we turned onto Breakwater Lane.

"But, Hope, don't you want to run it by someone just once?" Sam asked. "Just to make sure it sounds the way you want it to."

"I can hear myself just fine," she said.

"You know an audience appreciates things differently than you hear it in your head," I insisted. "That's basic acting, Hope."

"It's not ready yet," Hope said.

"We're pulling into school," I pointed out the obvious. "How much more time are you planning on taking?"

"As much time as I need," she said, putting an end to the argument. I'm sure Sam was ready to go another few rounds, but I had other things on my mind. As we walked to the auditorium, the real worrying began for me.

I don't remember ever being so nervous about a performance before. I actually felt a little sick to my stomach. I didn't think throwing up onstage would impress Hartley Blackstone all that much. Then again, considering his long résumé, he'd probably seen much worse before. Not that that thought was helping.

As soon as we stepped into Hall Hall, Sam, Hope, and I split up. We were going to use every second possible to continue preparing.

We weren't the only ones.

The Drama Geeks were all spread throughout the auditorium sitting, standing, or pacing in whatever space was available. Mr. Randall had clearly known we'd all be early, as the doors were open by eight o'clock, even though our teacher was nowhere to be seen. Not that any of us were looking for him. We were all too busy in our own worlds, going over our monologues for the last, second from last, third from last, and however-many-more-from-last times we could fit in before Hartley Blackstone arrived.

I went over my lines in my head, only checking back to my script occasionally. If I didn't have them down yet, no amount of last-minute cramming was going to commit them to memory. I knew this from experience. I had them almost all memorized, except for a couple lines in the middle I kept dropping.

Most of us were only holding on to our scripts and checking back to confirm a line or two. From what I could see, only Alexis seemed to be studying her script like all the words were foreign to her. At the same time, she seemed the least concerned of everyone. Even her sister—who was sitting right beside her—had her eyes firmly closed as her lips silently ran through her part.

It's always interesting to watch how other people prepare for an audition. That's what this was, basically. We'd given up any pretense of it being an acting exercise or simply another facet to the Summer Theatrical Program. This was, quite simply, the most important audition of our lives.

No pressure.

So, why did I keep drifting out of my own rehearsal to watch everyone else when I was supposed to be going over my lines? I couldn't really help myself. Living theater was all around me.

Sam was going through her vocal warm-ups. Jason was doing some stretching. Those two usually did the most preparation out of everyone. And it showed in their performances.

Tasha Valentine was sitting with her eyes closed listening to her iPod. She looked to be in a state of relaxation that I was quite envious of. Meanwhile, Jimmy Wilkey was at the total opposite end of the spectrum, pounding Frappuccinos in between opening and closing his script as if he expected the words to change every two seconds. If ever there was an example of what Eric's little brother would eventually grow into with his own caffeine addiction, it was Jimmy Wilkey.

Holly was filing her nails, as if she wasn't concerned in the least. She probably wasn't either. That's just one of the reasons I both hate and admire her at the same time.

And our darling Hope was sitting with her new journal in her lap, rewriting her monologue . . . only five minutes before Hartley Blackstone was supposed to arrive.

Oops. Scratch that. Julie Blackstone was walking down the center aisle with a man who could only be her father at her side. I mean, of course he was her father. He looked exactly like all the photos I've ever seen of Hartley Blackstone.

Everyone in the auditorium stopped what he or she was doing to watch Hartley Blackstone make his entrance. And a grand entrance it was. The man swept into the room, standing tall with perfect posture. His head was held high in the air. His eyes were focused on the stage and did not waver. Not once did he bother to look at the students openly gaping at him.

We were speechless.

Let me pause for a moment to explain what a unique experience this was. Celebrities are nothing new to us here on the left coast. Heck, several of the Orion Academy parents are major movie stars in their own right. (Not mine, mind you.) We see famous people all the time walking their dogs along the beach, going for coffee at Starbucks, or just sitting at a red light on the PCH with their babies in their laps. (Okay, I only saw that once. And, oddly enough, it was right outside a Starbucks.) Celebrity sightings are nothing new, even to the most jaded of us. But this? *This* was Hartley Blackstone, the king of Broadway. The man who created more stars than the big bang.

We were all suitably impressed.

Miss Julie introduced her father to Mr. Randall and we continued to watch as they exchanged a few words. I can't imagine I was the only one trying to read their lips. I failed, but you have to give me points for the effort. The conversation was brief, and the two Blackstones quickly took seats at the end of the first row while Mr. Randall waved us all to the front of the auditorium.

As one, we moved toward him, slowly so as not to look too eager, but somehow managing to appear even more excited than if we had run there. We filled in the seats around the Blackstones, careful not to get too close for fear of coming across as too pushy. Even Holly, who had made a beeline for a seat in the front row, kept a few empty spots between her and the theatrical genius.

Noticing that the auditorium seemed to be leaning a bit house right, Mr. Randall took a few steps over toward us to address the students. He said a few words about Mr. Blackstone and his career. To be honest, I don't think I heard anything more than a dull buzz. I was about to audition for the one and only Hartley Blackstone. Who cared what my teacher had to say at the moment?

Sorry, Mr. Randall.

I guess the formal introductions were done, because everyone around me suddenly burst into applause. I joined them as the master thespian stood up and gave a half bow. Instead of moving up beside our teacher, Mr. Blackstone mounted the small staircase that took him onstage. Although pretty much all of us were still seated house right, he stood front and center to address us.

"The theatre," Blackstone announced before taking a long, dramatic pause.

(*Aside*: While we're pausing, you may have noticed I switched up on how I usually spell "theater." You see that I'm spelling it "theatre" here. Technically, either one is correct, though the "er" ending is traditionally American while "re" is usually European . . . or American Pretentious. I don't know, but there was something about the way Blackstone spoke that made the latter spelling seem more appropriate.)

My, but he was taking a long, dramatic pause.

"The theatre," he said again as if we weren't hanging on Every. Single. Word. "Is a cruel mistress. One day, she can be a painted whore with her rouged face and her come hither expression showering you with her love and attention." *Oh my.* "And the next, she can turn her back on you, leaving you cold and alone in the silence of a disenchanted audience. Why any of us would choose this existence is beyond even the best scholars." Personally, I think it has something to do with money and fame. (And maybe a bit of a selfish narcissism that craves the attention. But I'm no scholar.) "Yet, time and time again, we do," he continued. "We answer the call of the greasepaint and are mesmerized by the beckoning stage lights. It is who we are. It is . . ."

He looked out at us like he was waiting for something. Meanwhile, we were waiting for the rest of his sentence. Sam,

Hope, and I shared a glance. We weren't sure if he was a lunatic or a genius or both. Either way, he was Hartley Blackstone, so we did what was expected in this situation: We applauded.

The auditorium echoed in boisterous applause. I was pretty sure we weren't the only ones who didn't have an idea what he was talking about, but it didn't matter. We were about to perform for the chance to be accepted into his summer acting program in New York. If he wanted to stand there all morning while we applauded, we'd do it, if only to increase our chances.

And, okay, Alexis was too busy laughing to actually clap, but what did she know about theater . . . or *theatre* for that matter.

After several bows, I guess he'd had enough. Blackstone raised his hands, like an orchestra conductor, and silenced the room. "Let the auditions begin," the artist said before descending the staircase. When he reached the bottom step, his daughter stood and joined him as they walked halfway to the back of the auditorium and took seats in the middle of the row.

"Thank you, Mr. Blackstone," Mr. Randall said as he stepped back in front of his class. We were all trying to focus on our teacher, but our heads kept twisting back to see what Mr. Blackstone was doing. As one might expect, he was just sitting there waiting for us to start.

"All right," Mr. Randall said, checking his watch and then looking to the back of the auditorium. "We're running a couple minutes early, but do I have any volun—"

"Me!" Hope shot out of her seat, putting way more enthusiasm behind her waving hand than I had ever seen from her before. Certainly more enthusiasm that I had seen from her all week. Sam and I looked at each other as our friend pushed past us to get to the aisle. We were not ready for what was about to happen.

At this point, I should mention Hope's choice of apparel for her scene. We don't usually dress in costume for monologues. And, if you didn't know Hope, you might not have realized that she was, in fact, in costume. While it was true that she was still sticking to her almost all black Goth-Ick style of dress, it was the name brands plastered across her clothing that tipped me off to what she was up to and the exact subject matter of her monologue.

Hope was dressed in black Hollister jeans, a black Hollister T-shirt, and a black Hollister baseball cap. I knew this because each piece had a colorful logo emblazoned on it to make sure you caught the name. Her contacts were a shade of gray that seemed quite familiar to me. In fact, there was a definite air of familiarity in her entire guise—one that matched a certain ex-boyfriend who shall remain nameless.

Before Hope could mount the stage, we heard the rear door to the theater open.

"Sorry we're late," Coach Zach called out as he walked in with the soccer team.

The soccer team?

"What are *they* doing here?" Hope yelled.

"They always come to see our performances during the summer program," Mr. Randall said. "Just like we always help with their scrimmage."

Bedlam.

Pure and utter bedlam.

This was not some performance. It was an audition. A fact that the majority of students found the need to remind Mr. Randall of, at a rather increased volume. It took about a minute for Mr. Randall to regain some control. He had managed to bring us to a small roar as the soccer team filled in rows in the center of the house.

"We can go if it's a problem," Coach Zach said before the guys sat.

Mr. Randall was torn. "Well—"

Mr. Blackstone cleared his throat, bringing utter silence to the room. We all turned in his direction. "This is theatre," he reminded us. "It is meant to be performed in front of an audience. If your students are unable to present their monologues in such a manner, then I do not feel that they would be right for my program."

That pretty much put an end to that.

The soccer team silently took their seats.

Without another word Hope walked center stage and looked out toward the audience. Sam and I both clearly saw her glance in Drew's direction. We were both shaking our heads and mouthing *no* to her. She could not do what she was about to do. I still had no idea what her monologue was about, but she was *not* going to do an impression of Drew. It would've been bad enough to do it in front of the Drama Geeks, but to do it in front of the soccer team and Drew himself? That would be a nightmare.

She wouldn't do it.

She couldn't do it.

Could she?

"Hi, my name is Hope Rivera," she said. Then she took a silent beat that about matched Blackstone's earlier dramatic pause in length. It was so bad that Mr. Randall leaned forward like he was about to check on her. I guess he figured she was suffering from stage fright or something. I almost thought she was too. I've never seen Hope look uncomfortable before—in *any* situation, much less onstage. From my seat, I could see a dozen different emotions flashing on her face during the length of her pause. Fear. Indecision. Anger. Love?

Sam and I looked at each other again, silently wondering if we should say something.

Hope finally found her voice. "I had originally intended to perform a piece that I had written myself. However, I'm not quite happy with it yet. So I've decided to go with a monologue from the nurse in *Romeo and Juliet*."

I doubt that Mr. Blackstone could have cared less about the change in program. I, however, was thrilled that she had used some restraint. Still, I was dying to hear what she had been working on almost all week. If only because I suspected that it might give us a clue what Hope and Drew had broken up over.

Hope launched into her monologue. It was the same one she had performed in our acting final in drama class at the end of the school year, so there weren't any real surprises. It was a rather lackluster way to start things off if you ask me. Not that she wasn't entertaining. No one does agitated older women better than her. Even though we had all seen her do the same performance a couple weeks before, Hope had managed to find a different approach to the character to keep it fresh. Considering that she was dressed like a guy probably brought a fresh approach to the character too.

"And . . . scene," Hope said as she ended her piece. Even though we don't applaud for one another in an audition, I could tell that most of the people around me were impressed. Even Belinda was smiling in appreciation.

I can't say the same for Hartley Blackstone.

"That was certainly some character work," the auteur said. "Not necessarily *good* character work, but there really is no such thing as good character work if you ask me."

"Excuse me?" Hope said from her spot on the stage. Her defenses were already up.

"Let me ask you this," Blackstone said. "You have the opportunity to audition for a world-renowned theatre program, and you settled on a character piece? Something with broad comedy and no nuance whatsoever? What possibly possessed you to think that was a good idea?"

"Juliet's nurse is one of the classic theater roles," Hope reminded him.

"True," he ceded. "But all the mugging and the exaggerated gestures. Do you really consider that serious acting?"

"No," Hope said. "That's why it's called comedy."

But Blackstone hadn't heard her. "Though I guess with your body type, you won't be landing the role of leading lady any time soon."

"And what *exactly* is wrong with my body type?" Hope asked.

If there hadn't been a dozen rows between them I would have feared for our guest's life. I swear I saw Mr. Randall's career flashing before his eyes. But the fire in Hope's eyes was exciting to see.

"I will grant that it was an effective performance, if ill-advised," he said. "Hardly worthy of my program, but better than average for a high school production. Thank you."

Hope's mouth opened, but nothing came out, which is . . . unprecedented. I could tell she was just as confused by his criticism as I was. Though he was incredibly rude to the point of offensive it almost sounded positive at the end. At least as far as her performance as a high school student was concerned. Hope looked a little shell-shocked as she came down the stairs and took a seat beside Sam and me. Neither of us said anything to her. We didn't have a clue what to say.

"Who'd like to go next?" Mr. Randall asked.

Not surprisingly, there were no takers.

"Anyone?"

No one.

"Okay, then," he continued, looking down at his clipboard. "Ms. Valentine."

It's rare that Tasha exhibits outward emotion. She's usually rather even-tempered. But I could feel the stress and fear emitting from her like waves from the Pacific were crashing over the PCH and up the bluff to take us all out as she stepped onto the stage.

Dramatic, no?

She looked out at her judge, jury, and executioner and began her monologue.

And thus the carnage began.

Sticks and Bones

"Boring." "Flat." "Uninspired."

These were the nicest words that Blackstone used in his critique of Tasha's performance. He went on for a while about how she made the same choices over and over and over again. Personally, I didn't think her performance was nearly as repetitive as his criticism of it.

As the morning wore on, his vocabulary got more interesting, but not any nicer.

"Bromidic." "Prosaic." "Abysmal."

One by one we took stage and one by one he tore us to shreds. The guy made Simon Cowell look like Mary Poppins. It got so bad I could even see the soccer team cringing. I could be wrong, but it's possible that Blackstone may have even started making words up halfway through the morning because he'd run out of insults.

"Banausic!"

Jason was the first student to actually earn more positive notes than negatives. Mr. Blackstone found the "performance as a whole quite moving," but thought that Jason "relied too much on subtleties of movement that barely made it past the audience in the first row." Then he went on for quite a while on the difference between acting for a large auditorium versus a small space, picking apart Jason's monologue for examples. All the while, Jason was stuck onstage.

But I remind you, that was the positive critique.

He got right back into form when Mr. Randall sent a row of sophomores at him like lambs to the slaughter that ended memorably with Missy Weinberg's interpretation of Carnelle from *The Miss Firecracker Contest*. I think we all knew it was going to be a disaster when she walked onstage with a CD player.

The monologue started out okay, but it quickly devolved into a hot mess. I guess Missy knew that her acting alone wasn't going to be enough because on the last line she hit the music and broke out into a tap routine that didn't quite fit in with the mood of the piece. We were all slumping down in our seats by the end, waiting for the worst.

Blackstone took another long dramatic pause before breaking out in a self-satisfied laugh. "Dance: Ten. Looks: Three," he said with what sounded to be a fair amount of pride in his *Chorus Line*–inspired critique. "Acting? Even worse." Hers were not the first tears of the morning.

Our teacher cleared his throat. "Mr. Blackstone, I would prefer that you refrained from commenting on how you perceive the students look."

"Mr. Randall, she is playing a character in a beauty contest. I am merely extending a criticism that is appropriate to the chosen role."

Missy picked up her CD player and made her way back to her seat. Her friends were there hugging her and shooting evil looks at the man we had all respected only a short time ago. Actually, scratch that. It wouldn't have been so painful if we all didn't still respect his opinion. It was the man behind the opinion we were growing to hate.

The lowlight of the morning had to be Jimmy Wilkey, our intrepid stage manager who had never acted before in his life. It was a massacre. *Way* too ugly to repeat here.

But I'll try.

It started with the performance.

"I'll be doing Eugene from *Biloxi Blues*," he said.

And we're off.

Jimmy launched into the monologue at breakneck speed. His movements were just as frenetic. Racing through his lines, he missed every nuance of character. Every moment. Every chance to breathe. It was like watching theater cranked up on speed . . . or espresso, more likely. The words all meshed together as he tripped over his speech racing to the end. Or, almost the end. He ran out of breath before he could choke out the last word.

But what killed . . . what *killed* was the innocently open and almost eager expression on his face when it was over. Jimmy had no idea how truly horrible his performance was.

He was about to find out.

"What the hell was that?" Blackstone exploded, his New York accent coming out for the first time all morning. The carefully constructed theatrical facade cracked for the barest moment before he recovered. "Mr. Randall, if this is the kind of talent you wish to place on display for me, well, I simply cannot understand what is it you expect me to do here today. That was . . . there are no words. No words!"

And yet, Blackstone continued to go on for another minute with words you wouldn't find on any Orion faculty–approved vocabulary list. The only reason I suspect Jimmy did not collapse onstage under the weight of his critique was because he honestly had no interest in being an actor.

Even so, I give the guy props for being able to take such harsh criticism without crumbling.

Thankfully, we all got a little comic relief when Alexis stepped onstage soon afterward. Her "performance" could only be described as tragically delicious. Without even bothering to introduce herself, Alexis launched into her monologue from *Medea*. Or should I say *attempted* to launch into her monologue.

"Women of Corinthia," she said. "I mean . . . Corinth. Women of Corinth!" Then a long pause. "I would not have you . . . have you censor . . . cen*sure* me," she continued. "So I have come here . . . come here . . . supercilious!" She froze. Looked out at Blackstone. Then at Holly. Then up to the heavens. Back to Holly.

"Fuck it," she said and walked off the stage and right out of Hall Hall, hopefully never to be seen again.

"Finally," Blackstone said. "Someone please thank her for saving me the trouble."

Her twin sister, Belinda, on the other hand was surprisingly good in her monologue. Not only did she get the words right, she clearly understood what she was saying. Blackstone still ripped her apart, but she also seemed to take that better than anyone else had so far. Having never acted onstage before, I guess she was just happy to get it over with.

That left, Sam, Holly, and me for last.

"Mr. Randall," Holly said. "I would be happy to go next."

"Okay," our teacher said. Since there were only three of us left, it wasn't exactly noble of her to volunteer now, of all times. I could only assume that she didn't want to have to follow Sam's performance. Not that Holly would ever admit that, mind you.

I had no doubt Holly's performance would be fine, but it couldn't come close to the acting she was doing by just walking up onstage. She stood tall and moved with an air of confidence that no other student had since Hope first stood before Blackstone. Of course, it's possible that it wasn't an act at all; maybe Holly was really that poised. Not that I could imagine what that kind of confidence was like.

Holly performed the role of Ivy like it was written for her—which, we all knew it was. I've got to give her credit. She was near perfect as usual. Sure, I could sit there and pick apart her performance; how she played too much to the audience and didn't internalize things as much as she should have. But that would be petty of me. Besides, I figured Mr. Blackstone was about to do just that.

"Very nice," he said. That was the first time he had ever started off his critique with a positive comment. "This young lady is clearly the reason my daughter brought me. You all could learn a thing or two from her . . . Miss Mayflower, is it?"

"Yes, sir," she said demurely . . . I mean, *really* . . . demurely!

Let me wrap this up because I can't sit through it again. He was positively glowing in her review, but he did point out that some of the parts were forced, like I thought. He suggested she take some of the passion out of her piece and replace it with more subtle emotion. I'd like to see that from the emotionless automaton myself. Oh, now I *am* being catty.

He also suggested that she might consider adding a few pounds because her small frame was positively diminutive onstage. HA!

Holly left the stage with the same look of confidence that she had when taking stage. Sam's name was called next.

"Figures," Sam mumbled as she passed me. It was either going to be her or me, so I guess it did kind of figure. That meant I was going to be next. And last.

Great.

I was so worried about my own approaching dance with death that I hardly heard Sam's monologue, but what I caught was full of her usual brilliance. No one, not even Holly, can match Sam for pure energy when she takes stage. She becomes the character. It's like I almost forget she's my best friend when I'm watching her. She's that good.

Apparently Blackstone thought so too. "Now I see why Mr. Randall saved these two young ladies to go together," he said.

"An interesting study in acting techniques, I must say. In many ways, your performance was like Miss Mayflower's. You put every ounce of passion into your piece. Too much, at times. Consider holding back more. No need to force your audience to accept you in the part. Turn out to the audience more too. The few small moments you did have are almost too internalized. But, overall . . . impressive. I am glad your teacher kept you two young ladies for last."

"Actually," Mr. Randall said, "we have one more."

Great, *again*.

Everyone's eyes were on me because they knew I was to be Blackstone's final victim of the day. I stood, slowly, shaking like I was on a sugar high. Slipping past Hope, I stepped out into the aisle and made my way to the stage, willing myself not to trip over my own feet. I tried to match Holly's air of confidence, but I think I probably looked somewhat like I had smelled some bad fish.

"Fedora!" Sam whispered as we passed, reminding me that I had forgotten to take off my hat. I quickly pulled it off my head and handed it to Sam as I mounted the steps and took center stage.

It was one of the smaller audiences I'd ever performed for, yet one of the most nerve-racking at the same time.

"Hi," I said out to the auditorium. I couldn't look at Blackstone. I was too nervous. Focusing on Sam or Hope only reminded me of what they'd been put through. For some reason, my eyes locked on Drew, of all people. "My name is Bryan Stark, and I will be performing the part of Tom from *Glass Menagerie*."

"That would be *THE Glass Menagerie*," Blackstone called out. "Always use the *full* title of the play."

"Sorry," I mumbled. *"The Glass Menagerie."*

"And don't mumble," he added.

"Sorry," I said loudly and with something approaching clarity. I paused and refocused my attention back at Drew, then launched into the monologue. I started out heavy, so I pulled it back quickly, toning it down a notch. I paused dramatically at the point I had rehearsed, then kind of lost it in the middle, and may have dropped a line or two, but I think I recovered nicely. I did pretty well to the end, until I stumbled on the last two words and actually saw Drew cringe. Never a good way to end a monologue, but at least it was over.

That is, the part where I had control was over.

I waited to be torn apart.

"Thank you," Blackstone said with a curt nod.

I waited for something more.

Nothing came.

That was it? Where was my critique?

The confusion on my face must have registered all the way back to the cheap seats. I could tell that it was mirrored in the faces of most of the students staring at me standing alone center stage while Blackstone ignored me so he could share a laugh with his daughter over something. Hopefully, not me.

Mr. Randall was apparently just as confused about the snub. "Um . . . Mr. Blackstone, don't you have anything more to say to Bryan?"

The auteur looked up as if he had momentarily forgotten

that we were there. He seemed particularly surprised to see me still standing onstage.

"No," he said simply. "Not really."

Then he went back to conferring with his daughter. At least she had the common courtesy to shoot me an apologetic shrug, for whatever good that did me.

Mr. Randall cleared his throat. "Mr. Blackstone," he said tentatively, "are you sure you don't want to critique Bryan's performance like you did with the other students?"

Blackstone looked annoyed by the interruption. *So sorry that my abject humiliation is cutting into your day*, I thought as I shuffled from one foot to another. "There was nothing there for me to critique," he said simply.

What the *hell* was that supposed to mean?

"Now, if you'll excuse me," Blackstone addressed all the students as he made his way out of the row. "Thank you, all . . . or, thank you *some*. I cannot honestly say that I would like to thank you for all that I saw onstage today. I will be back next week to make my final decision. But I will say that I am most interested in seeing more from the two young ladies who performed last." Actually, *I'd* performed last. "The gentleman who did a piece from *The History Boys* and the young one who had a physical presence somewhat reminiscent of a monkey—you need to watch that, my young fellow." Gary is never going to live down his role in *Wizard*. "Yes. If we had callbacks, those would be my choices based on today's performances. But since your teacher has asked that everyone continue to be kept under consideration, I will say that the rest of you . . . keep trying. Who knows? You could surprise me next week." Then he laughed like he was making a joke.

He left Hall Hall without another word.

Me? I was still standing center stage trying to ignore the Drama Geeks and soccer players in the rows in front of me. All of them were turning their attention to different points in the auditorium to keep from having to look me in the eye. Drew was the only one with the courage to keep his focus on me. Too bad I couldn't look at him in return. I could actually feel the waves of pity coming off of them all. Well, pity mixed with relief that they hadn't been left standing onstage like me.

Les Misérables

You know how in zombie movies all the living dead come shuffling out of the cemetery, or the woods, or the fog with the same glazed looks in their eyes, moaning in despair, with maybe even a little drool coming out of the sides of their mouths? Yeah. That's pretty much what we all looked like coming out of Hall Hall when Mr. Randall dismissed us for lunch. Actually, he kind of dismissed us for the day, suggesting that we could either come back to the auditorium later to work on our scenes or we could go somewhere else entirely. My group was still too numb to actually formulate any thought so we went to eat and then decide on a game plan.

En route to the pavilion, Eric came up behind us and grabbed Sam. He didn't bother saying anything. He just held her. This earns him even more points from me than anything he'd ever done before. The rest of us were stuck standing trying to mind our own business, until Drew made a move toward Hope.

"I can't do this," she said.

He simply nodded and continued to the pavilion. After a couple more seconds of awkwardness while Eric and Sam kissed, the rest of us left them behind and went for lunch.

If ever there was a time when it was easy to tell the soccer team from the Drama Geeks, it was in the Kenneth Graham Pavilion that Friday afternoon. The soccer players, while respectful of our trauma, were talking, joking, and pretty much living like it was a normal day in Malibu. The Drama Geeks? Not so much.

Everyone was so stuck in their own worlds that there were pockets of total silence mixed in with the soccer guys' conversations. With the exception of Holly, who never met a critic that she bothered listening to, most of us were still going over what Blackstone had said about our performances.

Correction: I was going over what he *hadn't* said about my performance. What did he mean by not giving me a critique? Was I so good that there was nothing he could criticize? Somehow I doubt it. That left only one option.

That I was that bad.

Hope, Jason, and I grabbed a table along the back wall of the pavilion. Sam joined us a few minutes later, while Eric went to the other side of the room to sit with Drew and their soccer friends. We didn't bother to say a word as Hope made room for Sam beside her.

Eventually, the silence really did become deafening. I was so lost in my own thoughts that I totally tuned out everything around me. I guess that's what made it so much more shocking when the world came crashing back into focus, thanks to Hope.

"Who the hell does he think he is?" Hope blurted out, scaring half the pavilion.

I guess her outburst was kind of the verbal equivalent of a starting pistol. It signaled the end of the moping and the start of the righteous indignation. Every one of the Drama Geeks started griping about their critiques, their friends' critiques, and even their enemies' critiques. It was bordering on mass hysteria that I'm pretty sure scared more than a few of the soccer players. But *everyone* had something to say.

Everyone but me, that is.

Hope was all, "What's wrong with being a character actress? Character actresses are finally getting respect nowadays. Look at *Hairspray*. Look at *Ugly Betty*. Hell, I have a much better chance of getting work than that beanpole Holly."

At the next table, I heard Tasha going all out. "Flat? Flat! I'd like to flatten him!" This coming from a vegan who respects all life no matter how small . . . or creepy crawly.

Even Sam and Jason, who both had received mostly positive criticism, were engaged in comparing their notes trying to decipher what moments they had blown and which ones had worked.

But me? I had nothing.

And I wasn't the only one aware of that. Don't think I didn't see the pointed looks in my direction coming from the other tables. From people who would turn away the moment they saw me seeing them. Then, there were my own friends, who were so busy griping about their own perceived slights that they weren't even bothering to notice that I was not part of the conversation. Even Hope, who'd hardly put two full sentences together over the past week, was rambling.

Part of me—a *big* part of me—suspected that they were running on like that because they didn't want me to engage. They didn't want to have to deal with how I had been snubbed. They couldn't even come up with anything to say to me.

It took a lot for me to climb out of my despair spiral. "I couldn't have been worse than Jimmy," I finally said, not realizing it was out loud. I quickly checked to make sure that Jimmy hadn't heard, but he was across the room chugging on a bottled Frappuccino.

"Of course you weren't," Hope quickly said.

"But even Jimmy got a critique," I said with a low voice. "He was horrible and Blackstone managed to find some things to say to him. None of it good, but still."

"You weren't that bad," Jason said.

"Thanks."

"I mean—"

"It's okay," I said, cutting him off. I really didn't want to hear what he had to say. There was only one person who could help lift my mood. Oddly, she was somewhat quiet at the moment.

I turned to Sam. "What do you think I did wrong?"

Sam took a moment to consider her answer. I guess she was about to say something when her eyes suddenly closed into tight slits and her entire body tensed. That could only mean one thing: Holly was walking up to our table. I turned to see her standing behind me with Belinda.

"Wasn't Blackstone amazing?" she asked. "That man can cut right to the heart of a critique, can't he? Such a refreshing change from the norm around here."

"Do you want something?" Sam asked.

"A spot in Blackstone's program," Holly replied. "And, if I read the room right this morning, I'd say I'm almost a lock."

"I'd say you were something else entirely," Sam replied. "But is there a point to you talking to us right now?"

"Alexis took the car," Belinda blurted out to the table.

"Is she bringing it back?" Hope asked.

"How should I know?"

"You're twins," Hope said. "Don't you have some kind of psychotic link?"

"I think that's psychic," Jason said.

"I think she was right the first time," Sam mumbled under her breath.

"Anyway," Belinda said, turning to me, "Bryan, can you give us a ride home?"

I wasn't exactly sure how to answer that. Considering Hope's house was on my way home, a ride wasn't a problem at all. But I was more concerned about Hope's reaction to me doing her step a favor.

"Can't Holly take you?" Hope asked.

Holly sighed. That deep sigh must be a Mayflower family trait. Her sister, Heather, is an expert at it. "I told you she was going to be a hard-ass."

"Hope," Belinda said. Her smile never faltered. "You're going to need a ride home, anyway. I thought we could save on the gas. Holly would have to go like a mile out of her way."

"Perish the thought," Hope said. "But I'm not actually going home. We're all going out."

Once again, this was news to me. I have to say that my friends and I are very good at the ambush lies.

"Where?" Holly asked.

Hope, Sam, and I looked at each other. Frozen. So much for our talent with the ambush lies. Our minds were so full of Blackstone that we couldn't come up with anything.

"My place," Jason volunteered. "We're going to rehearse our scene. But we need to get out of here. You understand."

"Of course I do," Holly said, all sweetness and light. "If Blackstone said about me what he said about you guys, I'd want to get out of here too."

Okay. Considering Blackstone said nearly the same thing to her that he said to Sam, I wasn't exactly sure what she was getting at. Sam, however, took it extremely personally and was ready to throw down. "What's that supposed to mean?" she asked.

"I was just making a comment," Holly said. "The guy was kind of mean. Especially to you, Bryan."

How sad is it that the first person to acknowledge this out loud was Holly Mayflower?

"If I were you," she said, "I'd go right back to the auditorium and demand to know just how bad he thought you were."

Ain't she great, folks?

"He's already gone," I mumbled.

Both Sam and Hope looked about ready to leap over the table and throttle Holly on my behalf. Or to throttle Holly just for the heck of it. Either way, there was about to be some throttling.

"Thanks, anyway," Belinda said, pulling Holly away. I wasn't sure what exactly she was thanking us for. All that we'd done was exchange some open hostility, but I give her credit for being smart enough to get her friend out of there before the bloodshed. A catfight between Sam and Holly would be fairly even, but once you threw Hope into the mix . . . it would get ug-o-ly.

Still, it was nice to see these brief flickers of life from Hope lately. It was possible that she was coming out of her misery on her own.

"Thanks for the cover story," Sam said to Jason once the girls were out of earshot.

"No prob," Jason said.

"You don't really want to rehearse, though," I said.

"No," he quickly replied. "Actually, I kind of want to be alone . . . to think."

"Yeah," Hope said dropping the remains of her lunch. "I'm done." She wasn't even halfway through her sandwich, but I knew what she meant. My own sandwich had only about three bites missing. "Me too."

Sam and Jason agreed. Ignoring any childhood warnings about children starving in other parts of the world, we thoughtlessly dumped the remains of our lunches and left the pavilion with hardly a good-bye to anyone. In our own way, I guess that's how we were going to address our critiques (or, in my case, the lack thereof). We were going to ignore them.

We split from Jason in the parking lot and I aimed Electra toward the Pacific Coast Highway, heading for Santa Monica. Please note that "aim" is the correct phrase to use here, as beachgoers are always dashing across the road to get to their cars. You have to steer carefully to miss them.

We were still in primo beach time so traffic was light. Once everyone decided to head home, PCH would be a parking lot. Granted, it would be a parking lot with one of the most amazing views in America, but a parking lot nonetheless.

The ride was pretty quiet because Hope had shut down once again. Sam and I tried to fill the silence with some banter, but neither of us was in the mood, so we spent most of our time watching the ocean pass us by. And, well, I was watching for pedestrians. In the relatively light traffic it only took fifteen minutes to get to Sam's apartment building.

As we double-parked to let Sam out, we could see her mom, Anne, standing inside the security gate going through their mail. I honked hello, but didn't expect her to come running out to greet us. A simple stroll would have been fine. Maybe even a light saunter. But the running was a surprise.

I suspect her exuberance had something to do with the small piece of paper in her hand. It looked like a photo.

"Sam," she called out. "Postcard!"

"Huzzah!" Sam said, leaning out the window and grabbing the postcard. Her use of the word "huzzah" could only mean one thing; this postcard was Ren Faire—related. I tried very hard not to roll my eyes. "It's from Marq," she said, confirming that it came from her old Renaissance Faire buddy. Sam and her mom used to do the Ren Faire circuit back before Sam started at Orion. And they're not even embarrassed about it. Heck, they're actually proud to be a part of that unique breed of characters.

While Sam read us the latest happenings on the circuit, a car honked behind us. Loudly. And with a sustained blare. There really was no need since the street was way wide enough for him to go around.

"Bryan, you'd better move," Anne said. "That's the apartment manager. He doesn't like people double-parking in front of the building. There's a spot at the end of the street if you guys want to come in for a few minutes."

"Why not?" I said, pulling forward with the guy riding my bumper all the way down the street. I smiled politely at him as I took the spot that he would have gotten had he just gone around me in the first place. Sam's small building does not have a parking lot, so they were stuck with on-street parking, in an area where spots are at a premium. I could only hope that the guy didn't find anything until he was a couple blocks away as punishment for his angry horn. I fully believe in parking karma.

We hopped out of Electra and headed back to Sam's apartment where Anne met us at the door with a trio of iced teas already poured for us.

"Thanks," we said, taking the drinks.

"Bryan, I need to borrow your height in the kitchen," Anne said before I could get comfortable.

"Certainly." I followed her into the other room. "What do you need?"

"Can you get that bowl?" she asked, pointing to a blue bowl on top of the refrigerator.

I kind of looked at her questioningly, then reached out and grabbed it. To say that it was a stretch, would be a stretch. It was certainly within Anne's reach.

"Thank you," Anne said, then she added in a whisper, "How did the auditions go?"

Ah. That explained it. She wanted to know what kind of weekend she'd be having with Sam. Their apartment wasn't large enough for her to pull me aside and have the conversation without being overheard. Hence the subterfuge.

"It was"—I searched for a word that quickly encapsulated the experience I was trying so hard to forget—"ghastly." I went with a word Blackstone had used several times that morning. It was the one most stuck in my head.

"Come on," Anne said. "Be serious." Then, I guess she saw my face, because the smile dropped from hers. "Oh. That bad."

I nodded. "Sam's critique was actually okay," I said. "But I don't think she heard any of the good stuff, so I'd be on alert."

"Are you okay?" she asked.

I had to think about that. "I'm not sure."

She gave me a pat on the shoulder before sending me back into the living room while she returned the bowl to its perch on the refrigerator. Sam and Hope were sitting on the couch. Both of them had grins that were *way* scary. I'm talking the Joker from *Batman* scary.

"What?"

"We're being stupid moping around like this," Sam said. "We should go out and have fun. Life is meant to be lived."

I wasn't sure what had brought about this sudden change of mood, but I didn't totally disagree. Still, if she broke into *A lot of livin' to do*, I swear I would have hurled.

"We're having a girls' night out," Hope said. "You're coming with us."

I looked at them. I looked down at myself. "Um . . . I have a penis. I know neither of you have seen it and you're never *going* to see it. But I assure you, it *is* there. And it precludes me from attending any event where being a girl is specifically called out in the title."

"You done?" Sam asked.

"Yes."

"You're coming with us."

"Okay," I said. "Where are we going?"

Hope's grin actually stretched to inhuman proportions. "To the twenty-fifth anniversary DVD release party of *On Angel's Wings*."

The Goat,
or Who Is Sylvia?

Hope's dad was so thrilled to hear that we were going
to the DVD release party that he sprung for a limo to pick us
up at Sam's place and take us to the party, which was set up in
a huge circus tent right in the center of the Hollywood and
Highland Complex. That's a shopping and entertainment area
with stores, restaurants, a bowling alley . . . and the theater
where they host the Academy Awards.

Hope and I had to make a quick dash to the Third Street
Promenade to pick up a few things to wear first. We'd decided
to get into the spirit of the eighties, as the party invitation had
requested.

Hope went with the full-on Goth-Ick Madonna look with
the lacey black skirt and tank top, fingerless gloves, and some
crazy neon rubber bracelets. Just to be clear, she wasn't dressing like Madonna, she was dressing like girls who dressed like
Madonna in the eighties. There is a difference.

We didn't want to swing all the way back to Malibu, so Hope had to stay with the gray contacts. They didn't entirely go with the guise, but since Hope was the only person I know who regularly matches her clothing to her eyes, we doubted anyone else would notice.

My choice was practically made for me considering my general look and body type. Hats were popular in the eighties (though mostly on girls), so wearing my fedora was a given. A tight, white button-down shirt and straight-leg black jeans were the obvious choice. Even though this ensemble only served to emphasize my lack of musculature, it like, totally fit with the look I was going for. Radical, fer sure. Oh, and the best part—the *best* part—was the pencil-thin tie I found with a keyboard design. *That* made the entire outfit.

All Sam had to do was go into the back of her mom's closet to pull a few things and voilà, she was a vision in acid-washed denim. There was no doubt we'd be reminding Anne for years to come of what she had in her closet. And we now had the photographic evidence as proof.

The limo was the best part of the pre-party prep. I'd been in limos before. And this certainly wasn't my first Hollywood party. But there's something particularly exciting about the combination of the two; stepping out of a black stretch limo and onto a red carpet among the glitterati. It is indescribable.

But I'll try to do it justice.

The limo pulled in at the end of a line of limos and we pressed our faces to the glass to see what was in store. Kara had spared no expense in the party. There was no doubt in my mind that she and Hope's dad were footing the bill for this extravaganza. The studio behind the release would have probably just done a small in-store appearance with Kara signing copies of the DVD for a few dozen of her more ardent fans. Certainly they wouldn't think that the amount of money they'd make on the movie would justify the expense of a huge party that partially shut down Hollywood Boulevard.

On Angel's Wings was supposed to be Kara Bow's breakout role. The problem was that the movie was only big in a cult way and she was so tied to the character that nobody ever saw her playing any other part. She had a few poorly received movies after it, and quickly faded into obscurity. Unfortunately, with all her success behind her, Kara sort of got emotionally stuck back in the eighties, kind of like that mom in Bowling for Soup's song "1985."

She did name her daughters for a character on *Dynasty* and the lead singer of the Go-Go's after all.

Even though we knew that Hope's stepmom had a bit of a hopelessly devoted following, we had never in our wildest nightmares expected such a turnout for the DVD release. Don't get me wrong. *On Angel's Wings* was a massive cult hit with incredible kitsch value. Blaine's reaction alone was clearly evidence that a certain segment of the Hollywood community would come out to support it. But this response was way more than I'd expected when we finally got to the red carpet and stepped out among the throngs of flashbulbs.

I'm not one for name-dropping, so let me just say that before we even reached the party tent, we passed a pair of anorexic, coke-addled actresses, a closeted gay action-movie star and his secret boyfriend, and a celebutante heiress in the midst of a sex scandal. There were also a fair number of washed-up eighties celebrities, many of whom were named Corey. It was like the current and future casts of *The Surreal Life* all on one red carpet.

Hope's dad, the famed celebrity defense lawyer, Martin Rivera, had clearly called in more than a few favors to stock the party with A-listers. From what I could see of the guest list so far, it bore no small resemblance to a rogues' gallery from TheSmokingGun.com.

Then, there were the goats.

Before I take you into the party, I have to tell you about the goats. See, an army of goats plays a pivotal role in the climax of *On Angel's Wings*. (Don't worry, I won't even *attempt* to explain it here.) So, someone—probably Kara—decided that goats should have a pivotal role in the party. And that's why the red carpet ran along a petting zoo filled with more goats than I have ever seen in my life.

Not that I've seen all that many goats in my life.

"Uh-oh!" Hope said as she stopped us ten feet from the entrance. Her mood was immediately lifted by the tackiness of the spectacle, as I'm sure Sam had intended when she'd had the idea to come to the party.

"What's wrong?" Sam asked.

"I've peaked too soon," Hope said. "We haven't even gotten inside and I've found my highlight for the evening. The one thing that even a phalanx of goats cannot beat."

"Do tell," I said.

"There," she said, pointing to the sign over the door.

I guess it was all the flashbulbs that had kept me from noticing it before. A huge, two-story-tall cutout of Kara Bow looking as she did in the promotional poster for the movie was stationed in front of the entrance to the tent. To get inside, you had to walk under an arch that was—well, there's no delicate way to say this—formed by her legs. But the *real* highlight was the banner that the fifty-foot-cardboard woman was holding. It read ON ANGLE'S WINGS.

"A perfect example of why people should not rely on spell-check alone," Sam said.

"Oh no, didn't you hear?" I said. "*On Angle's Wings* is the sequel. Her twin cousin, Tri Angle, has to solve geometry problems to get back into Heaven."

We all shared a raucous laugh as we entered the party.

That laugh was cut off as soon as we were inside. The place was packed with the hottest celebs around, all dressed as if they were experiencing an eighties flashback. You couldn't swing a dead career without hitting someone with an entourage. But who would be the first person we saw as soon as we crossed under Kara Bow's legs?

Drew.

Confirming once and for all Walt Disney's words of wisdom immortalized in song and annoying animatronic children: It *is* a small world, after all.

"That's just the perfect topper to my day," Hope said, though it didn't come out sounding nearly as harsh as it could have. Our plan was starting to work. She was obviously soft-ening to Drew, and prime for Phase Two of our scheme.

Maybe his being at the party *wasn't* such a small world coin-cidence, after all.

The two of them stared at each other across the crowded room. But neither of them was willing to make the first move. Eric was beside Drew, trying to get his attention, while Sam was busy distracting Hope.

"Your dad is waving frantically," Sam said, pointing over to the stage.

Hope and I turned to see Mr. Rivera. He was dressed in a simple yet elegant suit of a style that could not possibly have been any older than last year. I wouldn't refer to his waving as "frantic," but Sam was trying to distract Hope so I'll give her a pass on that one.

"Didn't really get into the theme of things, did he?" I noted.

"He's only willing to indulge Kara so far," Hope said. "Usually about as far as his own reputation goes."

"I should go say hi," Hope said . . . and then she did.

Once Hope was gone, Drew stopped staring and made for the bar. Eric, meanwhile, came right up to us.

"What are you doing here?" Sam and Eric said in unison. Speaking of unison. Eric was coincidentally dressed in match-ing acid-washed denim. He and Sam looked like they were ready to start some hair metal band.

"I didn't know you were coming," Eric said.

"It's a party for Hope's stepmom," Sam said.

"Exactly."

Sam was forced to concede that point to Eric. "Why didn't you say anything about it earlier?"

"We just got the invitation this afternoon," he replied.

Showing her usually exemplary insight, Sam turned to me for the explanation. "Bryan?"

"Remember when you and Hope went into the dressing room so she could try on outfits for tonight?"

"Yeah."

"And remember how I offered to hold your bags for you while she changed?"

"I was wondering why you did that," Sam said. "You never want to hold our purses for us when we shop."

"Yes. I'm a guy. Do I have to keep reminding you of that?" I said. "Anyway. While I had Hope's bag, it's possible that I used her cell phone to speed dial Alexis to make sure that Drew wasn't going to be at the party since we were now going. You know, so there wasn't any awkwardness."

"Thus ensuring that Drew would immediately be invited to the party," Sam said. "Brilliant." She raised a hand to give me five.

Unfortunately, Eric was a few steps behind. Not that it was his fault. "I thought we were supposed to be keeping them apart."

"Oh, honey," Sam said. "I forgot to tell you. New scheme." Sam filled him in on what was up while I scanned the room for the evil stepsisters. I only found the glowing red hair of their fear-mongering leader, Holly, holding court over a bevy of admirers.

She must have the heightened senses of a meerkat or something because she like *felt* me staring at her and looked up. Her flirtatious smile faltered for a moment, before she turned it back up on high and gave us all a little wave.

After the three of us waved back, Sam turned her attention exclusively to Eric. Between prepping for the auditions, and Hope's situation, Sam and Eric hadn't spent all that much time together over the past week. Knowing that they needed their space, I made my way over to the bar, where I met up with Drew, who was nursing the last of a martini. They never card at events like these, so it's pretty much an open bar free-for-all, which explains how Drew Barrymore was in rehab by the time she was thirteen. I ordered a soda . . . with ice . . . and a little stirring straw.

It's not that I'm a total Puritan when it comes to a celebratory glass of alcohol or anything, but if I got back to Sam's house with liquor on my breath, Anne would kill me. And then she'd make me call my mom to explain why I wasn't allowed to drive home. Nope. It was safer to stick with soda. Besides, Blaine was possibly somewhere at the event and his reaction would probably be even more severe than Anne's.

He'd take great pleasure in finding some way to embarrass me.

Drew, meanwhile, made like a male version of the similarly named Barrymore and ordered up his second apple martini.

"You know," I said, "there's a fine line between a couple drinks at a party and starring in an episode of *Degrassi* about underage alcohol abuse."

Drew kicked back his drink in one gulp. "I'll keep that in mind."

Now that I was standing closer, I could see Drew hadn't exactly taken the eighties theme to heart. He was wearing a Hollister T-shirt, an Abercrombie & Fitch baseball cap, and what appeared to be American Eagle jeans. He was a veritable United Nations of guywear.

"Where's your costume?" I asked.

He tapped a pair of Ray-Bans that were resting on the rim of his hat. How very Tom Cruise of him.

It's hard to say that Drew and I stood in silence at the bar, since the venue was pretty rollicking at that point. But, he and I apparently had nothing to say to each other. I guess he was still mourning the loss of his relationship while I was trying to figure out my place as Hope's friend and his former best friend. Either way, our silence was one of the more pleasant conversations we'd had in a while.

Leave it to Drew to go and ruin it. "She doesn't have to run away from me every time she sees me."

"I don't really tell Hope what she does or does not have to do."

"All I'm saying is you can share that information with her," Drew said. "I'm not asking you to tell her to *do* anything." He ordered another martini and we glared at each other while the bartender made it. Drew's eyes were already slightly hooded so I could tell the drinks were having an effect. I guess we were so intent on staring each other down, neither of us noticed the large hand that came into the picture until it intercepted the freshly poured martini.

"Thank you," Blaine said as he tipped the glass to his lips.

Both of our jaws dropped upon seeing him. Blaine had taken the eighties thing on full force. He was dressed up like Mr. T, complete with ten pounds of gold chains around his neck and a Mohawk glued to his head.

"That's not my drink," I stated clearly and for the record.

"Whoever it belonged to, it's mine now," he replied, raising the glass in silent toast. "Now, where is Kara Bow? I have something I want her to sign for me."

I tried very hard not to wonder what exactly he wanted signed.

Thankfully, he got his answer quickly. The band stopped playing, the lights dimmed, and a smoke machine started spewing dry-ice clouds into the room.

Blaine took another gulp of the drink that formerly belonged to Drew. "This looks promising."

"Ladies and gentlemen," a disembodied voice echoed throughout the tent. It sounded very much like the voice of God from *On Angel's Wings* (aka George Hamilton). "Please welcome onto the stage a woman who sang her way out of the depths of Hell. Miss Sylvia Angel!"

Blaine let out a war whoop as everyone burst into crazed applause.

Alexis and Belinda stepped through the fog from the back of the stage. Never before did I realize how much they resembled their mother. I think it had something to do with them being dressed *exactly* like her character from the movie.

Alexis was—suitably—the fallen version of Sylvia Angel, dressed in a red leather pantsuit and a wig with hair sprayed so high that one could single-handedly blame her for global warming. On the flipside, Belinda was Heavenly Angel in a flowing yet incredibly short white skirt and off-the-shoulder white top. Her hair was gently feathered to the back of her head.

Hope stood beside the stage trying her hardest not to laugh. Her father had an arm around her, beaming up at the stage with pride, like he missed out on the joke. Hope wasn't about to fill him in on it.

As the Twin Twigs of Terror flanked the stage, the lights dimmed even more. Somewhere in the background, someone struck the first chord of Kara's lone hit song from the movie: "Open Up Heaven's Gates." And a huge spotlight lit the rafters at the top of the tent.

Sam and I locked eyes from across the room. No words needed to be spoken. Nothing could be said that would beat the visual. I swear to George Hamilton that as the opening notes rose to a crescendo, Kara Bow came floating down from the top of the tent on a shiny silver chain. . . .

But wait! We're not done.

She got *stuck*. Halfway between the rafters and the stage. Just hanging there. Swinging . . . ever so slightly.

It was *awesome!*

Alexis and Belinda were jumping up and down, trying to reach their mother, but only managing to swat at her feet. The tech crew was running around yelling for a ladder while alternately trying to fix the control board. In the ensuing commotion, one of the goats from outside snuck into the tent and made his way to the buffet table.

Sam, Hope, and I locked eyes across the room. We were all thinking the same thing. As if on a silent count we began singing "High Flying, Adored," from *Evita* while we enjoyed the performance.

Unfortunately, Hope's dad quickly ran to Kara's aid. He calmly picked up a chair and carried it onstage for him to stand on. He then grabbed her legs and lifted her body so that she was able to unhook herself. Within a minute she was down on the stage and breaking out into song.

The performance wasn't *nearly* as good as the entrance. Not that I was listening. Once the goat had been wrangled—after demolishing the dessert table—I turned my attention to the throng of partygoers who were busy ignoring Kara's performance and nearly dropped my drink.

Standing with his own bevy of admirers was the last person I ever wanted to see: Hartley Blackstone.

The Critic

"That was beautiful," Sam said, running up to me after Kara's song was over. "A truly stunning performance unlike anything I've seen onstage."

"And I almost missed it," Hope added. "This is, by far, the high point of the crappiest week ever."

There was a lull as they waited for me to respond. But I couldn't. Blackstone was just standing there with his daughter. Laughing. Like he hadn't destroyed a few dozen teens' dreams only hours earlier.

"What's wrong?" Sam asked.

I nodded in the man's direction.

"What is *he* doing here?" Hope asked.

"Carrying his torment through the weekend?" I guessed.

"No. I mean . . . he wasn't on the guest list. I know. My dad forced me to help send out the invites."

"Holly," Sam said with a shrug. "She probably made sure

that he'd gotten a personal invitation. Hand delivered. By a stripper."

I *knew* she wouldn't just sit back and rely on her talent to get a spot in his program.

In unison, the three of us turned toward Holly's table. I guess Alexis and Belinda had joined her right after the performance. And while Holly still had her admirers drooling on her every word, the other girls seemed to be focused on one male in particular: Drew.

"No freakin' way!" Hope said as she stormed over to the table.

"That worked faster than I thought it would," I said.

"Not if she winds up in jail for killing the steps," Sam said. We shared a brief laugh, before realizing it wasn't so much a joke as an inevitability, and hurried over to the table. We passed Eric as he was making his way there to join his best friend. He was wise to quicken his pace along with us.

"Oh hell, the gang's all here," Holly said as we reached the table a mere moment after Hope.

"I just wanted to come over and congratulate my *sisters* on such a stunning performance," Hope said. I could see Drew trying to shy away from the girls, but Alexis and Belinda had their arms intertwined with his and were keeping him locked tight between them. "My favorite part was when Belinda was jumping up and down after Kara, and flashing the entire audience her Hello Kitty panties."

"You know what they say," Alexis chimed in. "If you've got it, flash it."

Ugh. Some people really need to leave the banter to the professionals. Still, she was doing her damage by snuggling up closer to Drew.

"Clearly a policy you've taken to heart over the years," Hope said. "Is there any guy who hasn't seen your underwear?"

"Drew hasn't," Alexis said. "But maybe we can remedy that situation later."

Oh. Hope had walked into that one. And I was reassessing Alexis's banterability.

"Hey . . . no . . . I'm not . . . It's just . . ." Drew tried to pull out from their clutches, but he could not break free of their grasp, which is ridiculous because the two of them together weigh about as much as a paper clip. And they kind of resemble a paper clip too.

"Don't worry," Belinda said gently while she continued to hold tightly. "We're just playing around. The wounds are still fresh."

"You want to talk wounds," Hope said as she took a step toward the steps.

Eric interceded before anything untoward could happen. Not that it stopped them from their verbal jousting over poor Drew. Rather than enjoying the experience, the guy just looked like a wounded bird. I didn't get to enjoy it either, due to the voice suddenly speaking in my ear.

"Now's your chance," Holly Mayflower said, leaning closer to me than I honestly felt comfortable with. I hadn't even noticed her getting up from her chair and shaking off the random guys that had been surrounding her.

"My chance for what?" I asked.

"To find out what Blackstone really thought of your performance," she said, tilting her head in his direction. Hartley Blackstone was over by the bar, ordering a drink. It was the first time I'd seen him on his own since I realized he was at the party. Not that I would have done anything about it had he been available earlier.

"Leave him alone, Holly," Sam said, immediately on guard once she realized there was a side conversation taking place.

"What?" Holly asked. "I think Bryan deserves a critique. Everyone else got one. Don't you think Bryan deserves to hear what Blackstone thinks?"

In my defense, I knew at the time that I was playing right into Holly's perfectly manicured hands, but I couldn't help myself. I looked at my best friend with accusation in my eyes. I wanted to hear what she had to say to that.

"Oh, please," Sam said, backing down. "I'm not going to play this game. Bryan, Hope, let's go."

"No," I said. "I want to talk to Blackstone."

Sam put a hand on my shoulder. "Bryan."

I shook her off and pushed past her before she could stop me. "I want to hear what he has to say."

I continued to maneuver my way through the crowd, regretting my spontaneous decision every step of the way. I couldn't back down now. I was committed. There was no way I could veer off and run out of the tent like I wanted to. At least, not without coming off like a fool. Holly would have a field day with that one. Besides, it was already too late.

Blackstone had been handed his drink and he turned around to face me right as I stepped up to him.

I pulled my fedora from my head and twisted it in my hands. "Pardon me, sir," I said, feeling a bit *Oliver Twist*. "I don't know if you remember me from earlier today . . . at Orion Academy? I'm Bryan . . . Bryan Stark?"

"Bryan Stark," he said, searching his memory banks. "I think I once had a financial planner by that name."

Great. There's one possible future occupation if the acting thing doesn't work out.

"Bryan Stark?" he asked again. I wasn't sure if he wanted me to fill in the blanks or not. I gave him another couple seconds. Honestly, I was in no rush. *The Glass Menagerie?* Tom, right?"

I nodded vigorously. "Yes."

"I'm not so good with names or faces, but I never forget a performance," he said with a laugh.

"Good," I said with a little more enthusiasm than I had intended. "That's what I wanted to talk about. My performance."

"What about it?"

"Well, that's . . . that's kind of what I was wondering. You left without giving me a critique."

"Yes. I did."

I glanced back at my friends and enemies. They were too far away to hear what was being said, but they weren't even bothering to hide that they were staring right at us, watching for reactions.

"Um . . . could you?"

"Could I?"

"Give me a critique?"

He took a sip from his drink.

"Not really," he said.

"Well, why not?!" Yeah. I took a page from Hope on that one. Particularly with regard to the volume level. If the room hadn't been loud with conversation, I'm sure my voice would have echoed through the tent. By their reactions, I think Sam and Hope *did* manage to hear me several tables away.

There was one person whom I had no doubt could hear me. Alexis had sidled up to the bar to order herself a drink and eavesdrop. Now when I looked back, I could see that Drew was physically holding Hope back so she didn't interrupt to kill her sister.

I focused back on Blackstone in time to see the man shrug off my question. He actually shrugged! Though he did manage to tear himself away from his ever-so-interesting drink. "There was nothing there for me to critique."

"Dad," Miss Julie said as she came over to us. I guess she heard me yell too. "Maybe we should take this conversation—"

Blackstone waved her off. "Nonsense. This young man has asked for my opinion. My opinion must be given."

Any other time I would have snickered at his comment. I would have rolled my eyes back at Sam and Hope. I would have done any number of things to make fun of his obnoxiousness.

All I did was twist my fedora some more.

"Bryan," he said. "Some people are born with talent. They have a natural ease on the stage. As if the theatre is in their very blood. Others can be taught. They'll never be as good as those born with it, but with time, they will be acceptable. Your stage manager, Timmy, was it?" I didn't bother to correct him. "That boy does not have even an ounce of talent in his overly energetic body. And yet, with the proper teacher, and years and years of training, he could learn to make a passable game show host or some such."

I did not like where this was going.

"But, in my many, *many* years in theatre, I've come to learn that there is another breed of being," he continued. "One where it's not about talent. It is not about learning. It's about connection. With you, there is no connection. You move through the part moderately well. You remember most of your lines. But watching you . . . it's clear that you never turn off your brain. You don't have a feel for the role. It's like I can see the wheels turning when you play a part. I can read it on your face. It says, 'This is where I need to look sad.' And 'This is where I should take a step.' 'This is where I need to remember my next line.'" He laughed at his little joke . . . again. I'm so glad *he* finds himself amusing. Even Alexis wasn't smiling.

"The part you are playing is all in your head," he continued with a condescending finger tapping on my forehead. "No matter how much training. No matter how much you work at it. It will never be here." He laid a hand down on my chest. Somehow, I didn't think he was talking about my rib cage.

"But—"

"No," he said gently. "I've seen it before. I've seen it in some of the hardest-working actors I've known. It's not meant to be. You will never be an actor."

"Dad."

Blackstone addressed his daughter. "It's best that the boy learn now. Rather than wasting his life pursuing a dream that will never come to fruition. . . ."

I could hardly hear him any longer. There was only one voice in my head: my own. It was saying, "Don't cry. Don't cry. Whatever the hell you do, do *not* cry in front of everyone."

Then, it said something *far* more useful.

"Run."

And I ran.

From the bar. Toward the exit. Passing Kara Bow taking photos with a trio of goats with angel's wings strapped to their backs.

My mind blocked out most everything Blackstone had said, focusing on one line.

You will never be an actor.

Over and over it repeated as I ran. The tears were flowing freely and without restraint.

Out the tent. Past the goats. Down the red carpet.

A stable full of limos were herded together at the end of Highland. Every one of them looked exactly the same. Black. Stretch. Not a white limo in the bunch to make it easier to find the one I came in.

You will never be an actor.

I ran from limo to limo looking in the front window for our driver. It was a pointless exercise. Hope had dealt with the guy. All I'd seen was the back of his head. And I couldn't even remember what that looked like.

You will never be an actor.

I made it to the end of the stack of limos, still with no idea where the hell our driver was.

I heard Hope and Sam yelling my name. They were running toward me. Hope's cell phone was pressed to her ear. I heard an engine start nearby. I ignored them and went to the idling limo. It was ours. Hope had called the guy, telling him we were ready to leave.

"Are you okay?" Sam asked.

"What did that man say to you?" Hope asked.

"I can't . . . I don't . . ." I could barely speak between the sobs. I got in the limo, slid across the seat, and looked out the window, so my friends could not watch me cry.

The limo ride back to Sam's was painfully silent. They didn't ask me anything else. My friends knew I didn't want to talk about it. I didn't want to think about it either, but they couldn't keep me from doing that.

I wondered if Blackstone was right. Or maybe he was a bitter old man who just didn't understand my talent. Or maybe he had gotten me confused with someone else. *Timmy*, for instance.

But I knew. Somewhere deep down inside me, I'd always suspected. But never put it into words. It was why Sam was so hesitant to be in my group. Why Mr. Randall always focused on my lines whenever he worked with me. Never really getting into a discussion of my performance.

I was never going to be an actor.

Babes in Toyland

The weekend passed in a blur of misery and Chubby
Hubby ice cream (my comfort food of choice). My friends
called, several times, but I wasn't in the mood to speak to
them. Between their voice mails and e-mails, it was clear that
Alexis had done what she was best at . . . spreading the news
far and wide. Both Hope and Sam had heard about what
Blackstone had said. And even though both of them made it
clear in their voice mails that the man was one hundred percent wrong, I swore I could hear it in both of their voices that
there was a small percentage of them that may have agreed.

But that might have just been my paranoid mind at work. I
was beginning to doubt everything I knew. Blackstone had
turned my entire world upside down and sent me into a
depression spiral that lasted the entire weekend.

Monday morning found me lying in bed staring at the
ceiling.

It had been a rough night of tossing and turning while I tried to shut down my brain. Just like the two nights before. No matter what happy thoughts I put there, or how many stupid sheep I tried to count, nothing could switch off what Blackstone had said.

Don't get me wrong. I've always known I wasn't the best actor in the world. Not even the best actor in Orion. But could I really be *that* bad? I was one of the leads in the school show this past year. Granted, I was Scarecrow #2; the one that *didn't* have the solo. But I figured that was because my singing has never been the strongest. But acting's my thing. I've been involved in theater since kindergarten. Sure, I never had leading roles, but I was always out there as a supporting character. You'd think someone would have said something by now.

Or would they?

There was a light tap at my door. "Bryan, you're going to be late," Mom announced from the hall.

I moaned something noncommittal.

The door opened a crack. "Time to get a move on."

Moving on was the last thing I was prepared to do.

Maybe it was the lack of sleep. Or maybe it was the general malaise, but I fell back on the old excuse I hadn't used since elementary school. "I don't feel so good."

The door swung open, and Mom flew across the room. Her hand was on my forehead before she sat down on my bed. "You do feel warm."

The benefit of having a mom who is a bit of a hypochondriac is that all I have to do is plant the seed of doubt and she's ready to call an ambulance. On the flip side, she does tend to hover when I'm *really* sick, which can get annoying. Sometimes you just want to be miserable watching the soaps alone.

"Is it your head?" she asked. "Your stomach?"

"Yes," I moaned.

"Okay, you get some rest," Dr. Mom said as she rose off the bed. "I'll make you a cup of herbal tea."

"Thanks," I said as she left on her errand of mercy. Mom wasn't into the whole Granola Earth-Mother thing, but she swore by herbal tea almost as much as some moms believed in the healing power of chicken soup.

I heard footsteps approaching a minute later. It was way too fast for Mom to have made the tea already, and Dad was still in South Africa checking his blood diamond mines or something. There was only one other person who would be at our house this early in the morning.

"Good morning, faker," Blaine said as he dropped down onto my bed. The springs squealed against his weight as I bounced like a ship at sea in the midst of a tempest. I would have much preferred Mom with the teapot.

"I'm not faking," I whined from under my covers. "I am genuinely depressed. Therefore, I am taking a mental health day."

Blaine sized up the general mood and quit with the jokes. "You want to talk about it?"

"Not particularly."

"Fine," he said. "But you know you have a choice. You can either hide from your problems like a baby or confront them like a man."

"Thank you." I stuck my thumb in my mouth and pulled the covers back over my head, choosing Option A.

"Uh-uh," Blaine said, pulling the covers back again. "I said hide from your *problems*. Not from me. Now, get up. If you're not going to school, then you're helping out at the store today."

"Summer!" I cried. "I want my summer!"

"Work ethic!" Blaine retorted. "Responsibilities!"

Now he was being unfair. I help out at Kaye 9 all the time. I'd been putting in overtime there since way before child labor laws would have permitted. Okay, dressing up stuffed dogs in designer outfits isn't exactly the same thing as working in a sweatshop, but it still wasn't the safest of working conditions. I once got a nasty paper cut from a sale sign.

"I'm going to need that photographer's eye of yours today," Blaine said.

I yawned. "The camera's on the dresser."

"I didn't say I needed your camera. I said I needed your eye."

The fear of what exactly Blaine wanted to do with my "photographer's eye" got me up right quick. I was worried that if I didn't move, Blaine would just take the eye and leave the photographer behind.

I'm kidding.

Mostly.

Mom arrived with the herbal tea as I was getting out of bed. Before she could say anything, Blaine announced that I would be joining them at the store. Knowing better than to question Blaine on the care and feeding of her own son, Mom turned around and exited my room with him.

"You could've left the tea!" I called after them.

Knowing better than to keep Blaine waiting, I dressed quickly, and grabbed a fast breakfast and a reheated herbal tea. Then we all piled into Blaine's truck and made our way to Melrose Avenue. En route, I sent a text message to Hope's cell telling her that I had to help out at the store and apologizing for missing rehearsal. A few minutes later, I received a message back asking, "R U OK?"

I didn't respond, because I wasn't sure of the answer.

Once we got to the store, Blaine had me start out by moving around boxes in the stockroom. I had the distinct impression that this was some kind of punishment for lying to my mother about being sick when I wasn't. I'm not embarrassed to admit that I don't really have what one might consider a body that was built for moving boxes. Scaring off crows? Sure. But manual labor and I were not exactly old friends.

Speaking of old friends, my time in the back room did net a bit of a surprise when I opened a dusty box and took a peek inside. "I forgot all about this."

"What's that?" Mom asked as she came into the back room carrying an armload of merchandise.

I pulled the framed picture out of the box. It was a child's watercolor painting of a dog strutting a runway wearing a designer gown. The Kaye 9 logo was hovering above the dog's head. It was a pretty good for a piece of artwork done by a ten-year-old.

The picture had hung behind the register for the first two years the store was in business. It would probably still be there, but Mom hired some high-priced decorator to redesign the store once it started turning a profit. The first thing he did was throw out the picture. Luckily, Blaine had saved it from the trash.

"I always meant to take that home," Mom said. "I'd wondered where it got to. Why don't you leave it by the back door and we'll bring it with us when we leave?"

"Okay," I said, leaning the picture against the wall. It really was an impressive-looking piece, especially considering the age of the artist when it was painted. My eyes kept going back to it as I moved the rest of the boxes.

Once Blaine confirmed that I had moved every box in the back room, he had me work the register for a while. That was cool because I got to hang with the assistant manager, Flora. She told me all about her trip hiking around Machu Picchu in Peru. A pretty impressive trip for a woman in her eighties.

By the time I rang up my third sale of Mom's most popular new item—beer for dogs imported from the Netherlands—I was getting a little tired. And hungry. It was almost lunchtime. Since the store was empty, I figured Flora could handle the register herself, considering it was her job and all.

I took five to go in the back where Blaine and Mom were huddled over the books.

When Mom saw me approaching she quickly, though subtly, closed the book they were going over. Like I had any idea what the numbers would have meant. I don't know why they were being so secretive. Maybe it was a doctored second book and they were illegally laundering money for the mob through the store.

And maybe I have *too* vivid an imagination.

"Run out of things to do?" Blaine asked.

"I'm having trouble figuring out what exactly you needed my photographer's eye for. The register looks the same as always."

"I'll explain all while we pick up lunch," he said.

As we walked to the restaurant where Mom had already put in an order, Blaine spent an inordinate amount of time talking about how beautiful the day was. It was beautiful, mind you. Not a cloud in the sky. But since it was exactly the same as the day before, and the day before that, and the day before that, I couldn't imagine why he felt it was topical. Unless he was stalling about something. Only after we had picked up the food did he finally bring the subject around to what I hoped was the reason he had gotten me out of bed and assigned me the forced labor.

"How's your mom been lately?" Blaine asked.

Still didn't see what this had to do with my eye. "Fine."

"Does she miss your dad much when he's away?"

Oh no. My parents were getting divorced! It figured. All Dad's traveling for work finally came between them. Not that they ever seemed to have problems when he was in town. Actually, they were almost adorably cute together (blech). But still, it had to be hard on the marriage. They had finally decided to give up. And Blaine was the one who was having this discussion because he's good at breaking news to me.

"I guess," I said. "She does seem better when Dad's around," I continued. "And they talk all the time on the phone." I was hoping if I could sound positive enough, he wouldn't tell me.

"Has she been stressed much? About work?"

Questions about work didn't exactly fit into my divorce scenario, but once an idea is lodged in my brain, it's hard to make it leave. "Not really," I said. "Actually, she's been kind of excited lately. I've even woken up a few mornings and she was still up from the night before working in her studio."

Blaine finally smiled, which I took to mean that this conversation wasn't going to be about divorce. Good. I have enough friends with parents who are happily separated to know that it isn't the end of the world or anything, but still, I like my parents together . . . when they are together.

Blaine stopped us in front of the store. We could see Mom and Flora laughing about something at the register. For some reason, we weren't going inside yet. I didn't say anything. We had gotten salads and sandwiches, so it wasn't like our food was going to get cold.

"Kaye 9 has been doing really well lately," he said.

"I've noticed more of Mom's designs in the tabloids," I said. The first time one of Mom's creations was seen on a celebrity dog in *Us Weekly*, orders for that same outfit quadrupled overnight. Now, it was common practice for us to go through the supermarket rags to see if there were any other shots of her clothing on celebrity pooches so we'd know to stock up.

"We're making pretty good money," Blaine said. "And

you've probably noticed how busy we were this morning."

"It has been more hectic than usual," I noted. Some people might not think that a clothing boutique for dogs would get a lot of foot traffic. Those people obviously do not live in Los Angeles.

"Now that you're a senior, Bryan"—oh, we were finally getting to the point of the day—"your mom is going to need you to step up more."

"You know I'm always here when she asks me to come in."

"Stepping up doesn't mean doing what you're asked to do," Blaine said. "It means doing things without being asked."

I got what he was saying, but I didn't have a clue what it had to do with my present situation.

"Now, I don't know what's going on with you right now and why you feel like you have to hide in bed from it."

Oh, that's right. I never told him. Whoops. Odd how manual labor took my mind off my troubles. At least for a while.

"But I do know that if you wanted me to know, I'd know," Blaine said. "I trust that you're man enough now to deal with it like an adult."

"Yes, sir," I said. I don't often call Blaine "sir," but it seemed fitting.

"Now, what do you think of my window?"

Whoa! Did I miss something or did our conversation just veer off in another direction entirely?

I looked at Blaine, then at the window in question. Actually, it was two windows; one on either side of the entrance. Blaine changes the window dressing every month. June's theme had been, fittingly enough, the Dog Days of Summer. It wasn't an original title for the window, but it sure was an original design. He'd taken several stuffed dogs and placed them in Mom's beach-wear. But instead of putting them in a beach scene, he had bought a bunch of stuff at Staples and put them in an office setting. It was almost like he was making fun of businessmen who had to work all summer instead of taking a vacation with their pet pooches.

"It's pretty kick-ass," I said.

"Yes," Blaine said. "That it is. And I want you to remember that when you do yours."

"My what?"

"Your window," he said. "I'm letting you do the windows this month."

Stunned.

"But . . . nobody does the windows but you," I reminded him. "Not even Mom."

"If I'm going to expect you to step up, I'm going to have to trust you to be able to do things for me."

Oh, God, Blaine's dying.

"Stop looking at me like that," Blaine said. "I'm not going any-where." Did I mention: scary psychic? "It's just a window. And I don't want to see any stupid Fourth of July themes. Be original."

I examined the store window from every angle for a good half hour before getting down to the real work of deciding what would go in it. Getting to do the windows was a big responsibility in Blaine's world—a fact that Flora reminded me of several times once I was back inside. I think she was a little jealous. The one time she moved one of the dogs only a few inches in the display, Blaine had been so upset that he didn't speak to her for a week. For someone usually so calm and rational, even Blaine has a little drama queen in him.

I spent the next hour going over the store inventory to see what materials I had to work with. I already knew the stock pretty well, but I had never really put it all together in my head before. Thankfully, we had a plethora of stuffed animals from Fleischman Bros. Animal Emporium in the back that I could use as my mannequins.

After an hour that got me absolutely nowhere, my stomach reminded me that I still hadn't eaten. I grabbed my sandwich out of the mini refrigerator and sat down in the stockroom for a lunch break. Two bites into my sandwich, my eyes fell on the watercolor painting leaning by the back door. It really was a nice piece of art. You could tell it was painted by a child, but that didn't mean it wasn't quality.

My sandwich was forgotten. Inspiration had struck.

I grabbed the painting and ran out to the front with it. Blaine had spent the last hour dismantling the old window display while I had searched for the new one. I leaned the painting in one of the empty windows, then ran outside. The picture really popped in the natural light. I imagined that it would look even better when it wasn't resting against a plastic fire hydrant.

After another five minutes of staring at the window, Blaine joined me out on the sidewalk. "You might be onto something there," he said.

"I think I am," I said as I dashed into the store and to the stockroom.

I loaded my arms down with every single puppy mannequin that we had and brought them out to the selling floor. One by one I took the dogs around the place to find the most adorable and childlike outfits that would fit them. Little footie pajamas. Puppy-size sports uniforms and cheerleader outfits. Even a beanie with a propeller.

I placed one of every dog toy Mom stocked in the window stage right. There were squeaky toys and chew toys and interactive toys. I even left the plastic fire hydrant in and covered it with puppies. It was the doggie equivalent of the best Christmas morning ever in that window. I briefly considered breaking out the holiday decorations and going with Christmas in July as a theme, but that seemed too obvious. Blake was expecting originality here. I needed something *different*.

In my exuberance, I had used all of the puppies in the window on the right. I didn't notice that until I went back outside to see how it was progressing. The window showed the best dog party *ever*, but the other window sat empty. I could see Blaine watching me from inside. I gave him the biggest smile ever when I found my answer.

Running back inside, I grabbed a stuffed Jack Russell puppy and stripped him out of his denim overalls. He was one of the articulated animals, which meant I could pose him, and I did. I placed him in the empty window on the left, sitting on his rear and looking over at his friends. Alone.

I swear, you could see the sadness on his face at being left out. I felt almost cruel for taking him away from the party . . . until I reminded myself that he was an inanimate object and had no actual feelings.

I finished off the windows by hanging the painting in the crazy toy-filled window and going back outside to see how it looked. The poor little naked puppy was so sad over by himself while all his friends were at play.

I couldn't imagine anyone walking past the window without feeling guilt about neglecting their own dogs. My window would totally drive up traffic into the store if only to ease the consciences of the dog owners that shopped on Melrose Avenue.

If only I had brought my camera!

Blaine came out to join me as I snapped pictures with my phone. He took a good long look at the windows. I don't think I breathed the entire time. Finally, he nodded his head in appreciation. Sometimes a silent critique can speak volumes.

While we were standing there, a mother walked up to the window with her small child in a stroller. She stopped to see what we were staring at. I could see the child's tiny face as it turned from one window to the next. Back and forth the little head twisted as he took in the scene I created.

The little guy reached out to the poor little lonely puppy. Then he burst into tears. The woman soothed the child as Blaine held the door for her so she could go into the store to shop.

Once she was inside, Blaine and I regarded each other in silence.

It was entirely possible that the kid had just wet himself. Or that he was hungry. Or a dozen other possibilities. But my mind was focused on one explanation only.

My window display had made a small child cry.

Success!

Merrily We Roll Along

I slept well Monday night. Not because I had forgotten a single word of what Blackstone had said to me, or because the success of my window design altered my mood in any way (though I did do a spectacular job). I think the sleep came because I'd hardly been able to close my eyes since Friday. Exhaustion finally took hold and I was out shortly after *Access Hollywood* ended.

Which meant I woke up a tad earlier than usual. As I stared at the ceiling for the fourth morning in a row, I tried to psych myself up for going back to Orion. It wasn't easy, but when I pushed all logic aside, I convinced myself that there was a chance I could change Blackstone's opinion of me by doing some impressive scene work.

My monologue could have been a fluke. I wouldn't have been the first actor to let the pressure affect his performance. I did want to get into Blackstone's program, badly. If I could somehow manage to push through my insecurities, I could do a stellar scene, forcing Blackstone to reevaluate his critique and see me for the talent that I possess.

Was I being delusional? Quite possibly. But it got me out of bed.

An hour later, I pulled Electra into the Orion Academy parking lot right behind Sam and Anne. We exchanged awkward greetings, deciding to avoid the elephant in the lot since it wasn't the best way to greet each other after several days incommunicado. (A rarity for us, I assure you.)

While Anne drove off, I subtly glanced at Sam's neck to confirm that she was still wearing her unicorn necklace and, therefore, had not slept with Eric. She was. And she hadn't. "Have a nice weekend?"

"Please stop doing that," she said.

"Doing what?"

"Checking to see that I've got my necklace on," she said. "I'm sorry I ever told you what it would mean when I took it off. Any time I see you after I have a date with Eric, you're always looking at my neck like you're the Vampire Lestat getting ready to take a bite. It's annoying."

So much for subtle. "Sorry," I said.

"That's okay," Sam said, letting me off the hook. I could tell she was going for gentle in light of my meltdown the other night.

"What's the latest on the Hope/Drew situation?" I asked.

"Still morbid. Still depressed."

"Still 'Can't Smile Without You'?"

"That's what Eric says," Sam replied. "There was a glimmer of hope with Hope, though. We spent an hour on the phone bitching about Alexis on Saturday. But by Sunday, she was back to cold and aloof. She still won't tell me what she and Drew are fighting—or *not* fighting—over, but I think she's softening to the whole idea of talking to him again."

"Here she comes," I said as the purple people eater pulled into the lot. I guess the monstrosity of a car had sufficiently snacked for the morning, because only Hope and Belinda got out of it. Not that Alexis would have made a proper meal for any vehicle, no matter how small.

The girls split in different directions as soon as they were out of the car. I braced myself for Hope's full-throated defense of me as she walked up. Just because Sam was tiptoeing around the subject didn't mean that Hope wouldn't be all offering to kill Blackstone to avenge me or some such. Have to say, I might have been willing to take her up had she offered.

"Hi," Hope said.

"Hi," I replied.

"You okay?"

"I guess."

Hope nodded.

That was it?

No screaming in righteous indignation for me? No bold statements of solidarity? Not even one little, tiny death threat?

Man, this breakup with Drew really was affecting her.

But since she'd opened negotiations . . .

"Look," I said, "I'm sorry I bailed on rehearsal yesterday."

Sam put up a hand to stop me. "Don't even. Blackstone's an ass. I don't blame you for not wanting to come in."

I took a deep breath. The next part, I'd rehearsed on the way over. It was difficult, but it had to be done. "I wouldn't blame you if you don't want me in the scene anymore. I don't want to ruin—"

"Uh-uh," Sam said. "No way. We're a team. You are not backing out. I don't care how bad your acting sucks. We're stuck with you."

My eyes went wide. "*Et tu, Brute?*"

"Me too, you no-talent hack," she shot back.

"Diva!"

"Drama queen!"

"Holly Mayflower!"

"Now, that was cruel and uncalled for," she replied.

"And they say I'm the weird one," Hope added.

"Feel better?" Sam asked me.

"No, but we can go inside," I said. Actually, I did feel somewhat—well, not *better*, but not as bad. Sam and I live by the credo that we can survive anything, so long as we have the ability to joke about it.

"Where's Alexis?" I asked Hope as we went inside.

"She bailed," Hope said. "Hasn't been back since Friday. Don't think she's coming back at all."

Okay. That did make me feel a *little* better.

"Oh, I almost forgot," I said. "Blaine let me design the windows at Kaye 9."

"Get out!" Sam said, giving me a congratulatory—and painful—punch in the shoulder.

"Nice!" I said, rubbing my arm. As we roamed the halls to all of our lockers I filled them in on the story of my window design, embellishing details only when absolutely necessary. I accompanied the tale with visuals, showing them the pictures I'd taken with my phone.

"Ohhh," they said. "Ahhh."

"And the window totally made a small child cry," I added.

"Congratulations," Sam said as we reached the auditorium.

"Thank you," I said, almost forgetting that I was supposed to be miserable. Reality slammed me right back into place as soon as we stepped into the auditorium.

All eyes were on me as we walked down the aisle. And not in a good way either. Whispered conversations and awkward glances followed me every step of the way. It could only mean one thing.

"Alexis really is good at what she does," I said as we reached the front row.

"Sorry," Hope said. "I should have warned you."

"Everybody knows?" I asked. I knew Alexis was good with the gossip, but I never thought she was *that* good.

In answer to my question, Jason came up to me and said, "Screw him. We've got work to do."

It was one thing for Sam and Hope to support me. They were my best friends and all, so it was kind of an unconditional love thing. But Jason's response was entirely unexpected and quite appreciated. My mood was momentarily lightened, until I saw the daughter of the dream destroyer enter from backstage.

Miss Julie faltered a bit in her step when she saw me. She gave me a solemn smile, like she was trying to apologize for her father, but didn't know exactly how to say it. I smiled back in the most reassuring way that I could. I doubt she bought it.

I doubt anyone bought my brave act. Then again, considering how bad I apparently am at acting, that shouldn't be a surprise.

The only person who didn't seem to know what was going on with me was Mr. Randall. Either that, or he just had larger concerns at the moment, as I was about to find out.

"Everybody up onstage," he said, clapping his hands together twice.

Never before have I seen a group of students so reluctant to take the stage. It was as if we'd all been taken over by those zombies again. Then I remembered that I wasn't the only one Hartley Blackstone had destroyed with his criticism the other day. Mine was just the most vicious.

Lucky me.

"Come on," Mr. Randall cheered. "I don't want a repeat of yesterday. Energy people. Energy." Boy, he was really pouring it on. Our teacher wasn't easily excitable. So, for him to be cheering and clapping . . . well, something had to be up.

I got into position beside Sam while the rest of the group continued to lurch their way onstage. "Tell me it wasn't this bad yesterday."

"Worse," she replied.

It was the most miserable group of actors I'd ever seen. And I have to say that I was kind of annoyed. I was supposed to be the one getting all the pity. I mean, I was the only person told that he was never going to be an actor. How dare they be all selfish and self-absorbed!

"All right, let's start with some movement exercises," Miss Julie announced with way more enthusiasm than I felt was necessary. Then again, considering how we were all moving during the exercises, I guess it didn't hurt that someone in the room showed some energy. The rest of us . . . well, it looked like we were preparing for the next zombie uprising.

And lurch, one, two, three. Moan, one, two, three.

After fifteen minutes of stilted movement, Mr. Randall gave up and had us sit on the stage floor so he could fill us in on the day's schedule. In the morning we'd split up to work on our scenes in the different rooms he'd assigned us. "And the afternoon will be spent helping the soccer team prep for tomorrow's Soccer Clinic and Scrimmage," he said.

A collective moan rose from the zombies.

"Hey," Mr. Randall said, "they support us. It's only right that we support them too."

No one bothered to remind our teacher that the last time the soccer team supported us we were all embarrassingly critiqued to shreds in front of them.

"Here's the deal," he continued, assigning us our roles for the afternoon and the following day.

The Soccer Clinic and Scrimmage is this, like, *huge* event for Orion Academy. Kids in youth soccer camps from around the area come to learn the basics from our star players in the morning. Then, in the afternoon we all get to watch a scrimmage between the Orion Comets and our rivals, the St. James Knights. It's a total fair atmosphere that's usually kind of fun. But considering it meant taking time away from our rehearsals, we were, understandably, less enthused than usual.

And some of us were as incorrigible as a Von Trapp child.

Holly pulled Mr. Randall aside after he dismissed us to go to our rehearsal rooms. Sensing trouble, my group hung back to listen in. "Mr. Randall," she said. "Gary, Bel, and I would like to be excused from helping out with the scrimmage."

"I'm sorry, Holly, but you know that's what you signed on for when you joined this program," Mr. Randall said with teacherly diplomacy. "It's the same every year."

"Yes, but we don't have the chance to audition for Hartley Blackstone every year," Holly reminded him.

"If I excuse your team, I'll have to excuse all the teams, Holly," he said.

"No, you don't," Holly said. "I think Hart made it pretty clear who he was interested in." When did he become *Hart*? "You only have to excuse those groups."

"Holly, everyone has an equal chance at being accepted into Mr. Blackstone's program."

"I'm sorry, Mr. Randall, but that's just not true," she replied. "I think if we focus on putting our best work forward for Hart, then it will only serve to make Orion Academy look better as a theatrical training ground."

Only Holly could make selfishness look magnanimous.

I couldn't entirely disagree with her. Largely because I wanted the extra rehearsal time. Blackstone had made it fairly obvious that he was most interested in seeing Sam and Jason, and I was a part of their team.

"Holly, your team can continue working through lunch if you choose, but everyone is to meet back in the auditorium at one. Now, go make use of the time that you have."

Holly looked properly chastised, but I'm pretty sure that her devious mind was working on Plan B even as I grabbed my things and accompanied my team to Anne's classroom. I figured I had a lot to catch up on, having missed yesterday's rehearsals.

Once we moved all the desks to one side of the room to give us some floor space, Sam quickly ran me through the blocking. As I had expected, they laid out the entire scene in my absence. If you ask me, it was pretty stilted. At one point, they had me walking through the scene for no reason other than they needed me out of the way. So there I was, walking aimlessly and looking at the sights. I would have said something, but considering I had bailed on them I didn't really think it was my place. Besides, who was I to question the people who had a future in acting?

"I brought this to help set the mood," Jason said as he pulled out an iPod boom box and hit play. Forest sounds filled the room.

"Sound effects?" Hope asked.

"Only for inspiration," he explained. "We won't actually use it on Friday."

"Good to know," Hope said.

"I think we're ready to start," Sam said once we'd gone over all her notes for me.

We all took our opening positions and began the run-through. As usual, Sam already had her part memorized. Hope and Jason only had to rely on their scripts occasionally, while I had my head down, reading, the entire time. I would have been better prepared if I could have managed to look at my script once over the long weekend.

The scene from *A Midsummer Night's Dream* that Jason had picked took place in the forest where most of the play is set. It came after the fairy creature Puck enchanted Jason's and my characters so that we thought we loved Hope's character instead of her best friend—whom we *really* loved—who was, naturally, played by Sam. It's all about mistaken identities, misplaced loyalties, and good old-fashioned jealousy. Comic gold, I tell you.

So, why couldn't we find the funny?

"That didn't feel right, did it?" Jason asked when we were done.

We all slowly shook our heads, but didn't really say anything. It wasn't exactly one of our best performances.

Actually, scratch that. It was totally lame.

It was clear what had happened while I was gone. Sam, Hope, and Jason each had something they wanted to prove with the performances. They didn't bother to think about the scene as a whole. It was nothing more than a series of moments for each of them to shine. Sam had chosen specific beats to push, while Jason had his own matching agenda. And Hope . . . well, Hope was just miscast.

There's no question that Hope is a great actress and she will be able to perform any role when she gets older. But right now, her strength is with her personality: big and brash parts. She kept trying to be bold when she was supposed to be shy. I get that she had something to prove to Blackstone, but I wasn't sure this was the time to be taking chances.

Naturally, I didn't say anything to anyone. Who was I to criticize? I just kept walking through my part and doing what I was told.

And I was told a lot.

"No. Say it like this."

"No. Do it like this."

"No. You should let me really smack you in the face. It looks more real."

But I wasn't the only one. While Sam, Hope, and Jason were criticizing me, they were also critiquing themselves. There was more self-doubt and more second-guessing than I had ever experienced in one rehearsal. To think that the opinion of one man—and granted, he is a theatrical genius—threw us all into such a tailspin was certainly saying something.

Then again, it kind of made sense. We do go to a school where everyone who auditioned for the spring show was cast in a major part so that no one felt left out. Growing up in Malibu, my friends and I do tend to be sheltered from any real criticism. Even Mr. Randall's critiques during class are couched in positive comments to ensure that no students—

and more important, no parents—are offended to the point where Mr. Randall's job would be in jeopardy. Maybe that's why everyone was taking the criticism so badly. That, combined with the fact that these auditions meant so much . . . well, I guess we were all feeling the pressure.

"I hear David Beckham's going to be guest referee tomorrow," Jason said at the end of our last run-though.

"I wonder if Posh is going to show," Sam said.

"If she does, I imagine the paparazzi will be out in force," Hope added.

They looked at me. Waiting for me to add a line. "Then we'd better make sure we look especially good tomorrow."

Obviously, we'd found our chosen method for dealing with the pressure.

We were going to ignore it.

Crimes of the Heart

I can't believe I got bathroom duty. Then again, I couldn't have come up with a better metaphor for the week I was having. At least I wasn't alone. Sam was stuck with me as we escorted the kids through the small forest between the soccer field and Orion's main campus on bathroom runs throughout the morning. It's not like they could really get lost. It wasn't really a forest so much as it was a large patch of trees. Still, we didn't need any kids taking a wrong turn and wandering off the bluff. At least Sam kept us entertained by leading us all a rousing rendition of *Heigh-ho, heigh-ho, it's off to pee we go*.

The Soccer Clinic and Scrimmage was an even bigger event than the one last year. Parents, Orion students, and assorted guests were all over the place among the actual kids from soccer camp that the event was intended for. I guess it was true that David Beckham was coming for the scrimmage part because the paparazzi was set up before we'd even arrived that morning. I would have preferred to spend the day rehearsing, but there was no doubt the soccer team needed the extra hands. Kids were running around everywhere. And they all had to pee like a dozen times each before we'd gotten through lunch.

When we reached the bathrooms, Sam and I took a quick head count to make sure none of the kids was eaten by a coyote on the way through the woods. Nope. All there. We let them go in on their own as there was only so far that the escorting was necessary.

"Let's run lines," Sam said while we waited. Leave it to her to try to wring a rehearsal out of every minute.

"I don't have my script," I said.

"You don't have the lines down yet? Bryan, we go on in two days. You *have* to get them down." Her intensity level was somewhat disturbing, though understandable.

I shied away from her. "I will. I promise."

"Sorry," Sam said. "I'm getting a little stressed and feeling out of control."

"That seems to be going around," I said as a pair of stragglers made their way out of the trees. Jimmy Wilkey was escorting a familiar young face toward us. They were passing a Frappuccino between them.

"Hi, Sam! Hey, Bryan!" Eric's brother, Matthew, said as they reached the rest area. "This is such a great day! I'm having the *best* time. And I got to meet your friend Jimmy. He walked me here and let me have some of his Frappuccino, which was really nice. And I made sure I thanked him like Dad always tells me I should do. He's a pretty cool dude."

Probably the first time anyone had ever called Jimmy a cool dude.

"Oh, Jimmy, you shouldn't have done that," Sam said, taking the bottled coffee drink out of Matthew's hands and handing it back to Jimmy.

"I'm sorry, Sam. I didn't know. Matty said that it was okay. But I guess I shouldn't believe everything I hear. Especially from a kid. That's good advice in life, you know. I guess I am too trusting. But I'm really, really sorry, and I won't do it again."

Yep. Eric Whitman's brother was totally going to grow up to be Jimmy Wilkey. I took a particular amount of pleasure in picturing that.

"Don't worry, Jimmy," Sam said, trying to hold back the laughter like I was. "It's not that big a deal."

"Okay, thanks," Jimmy said. "I mean it. Thanks. Sorry."

Jimmy vibrated back to the soccer field, finishing his drink on his own.

"How's your plan going with Hope and Drew?" Matthew asked. He was bouncing up and down on the balls of his feet.

"What? Your brother's not keeping you in the loop?" I asked.

"I ask, but he always tells me to shut up."

I looked at Sam. "That's not nice."

"Well, I do talk a lot," he admitted.

Oh.

"I saw them together on the field earlier," Matthew added.

"Well, they weren't *together*, together, but they were together. On the same field. But I didn't expect to see them there, you know. Weren't you going to keep them apart?"

"We've moved on to Phase Two," I said. "It's progressing quite nicely."

"Cool," Matthew said.

"Cool," I agreed.

While Matthew joined the rest of the bathroom contingent, Sam asked, "What is going on with our scheme? Do you have any plans for Hope and Drew today?"

"No need. The twigs can handle it on their own from here." I pointed to the parking lot. "Check it." Alexis was trying to pull something out of the back of the purpmobile, flashing her butt to all passersby. I guess one of the perks to ditching the Theater Program was that she didn't have to help with the Soccer Clinic and could come late for the game.

"Looks like Drew's going to have his own little cheering section," Sam said.

"That should annoy Hope enough on its own," I said.

"Are you sure?" Sam asked. "Because we can always have something ready to go in reserve."

"Boy, you are stressed."

"I know," Sam said. "Aside from being worried about everything I do, I'm afraid that Hope being all morbid and depressed is going to affect her performance. And that won't be good for any of us."

"She pulled it together for the monologue," I reminded Sam. "She can do the same for the scene."

"I'd feel better if we could get her and Drew back together," Sam said. "I mean, I think they should be together for themselves, but—"

"But if we get a better scene out of it, then it helps all around," I filled in the blanks. "Gotcha. And trust me. Alexis has got our backs."

We watched as our unknowing ally flagged down a guy to help her pull whatever it was out of the back of the car. If she worked Drew even half as much as she was working the guy, we would have nothing to worry about. Hope would never stand for that crap.

Once the last of our charges was out of the bathrooms, we performed another head count to make sure none of them had been flushed out to the ocean, and returned to the soccer field.

We had a few more round trips to the bathroom before the teams started to set up the scrimmage. Alexis still hadn't made an appearance and we were worried that we might miss it whenever it came. Each time we went back to the field, we saw Hope and Drew actively trying to keep their eyes off each other. I wasn't sure that either of them wanted to get back together, but it was clear to me that the period of estrangement was getting old for them.

"We hereby turn bathroom duty over to you," I said to a pair of tenth graders upon returning from our final bathroom trip.

"Thanks," they moaned. Hey. I had to miss the game for bathroom duty back when I was a sophomore. Not that I normally minded missing a soccer game. But this one promised to have quite a show with it.

The opening act began as Alexis came through the trees. She was wearing tight blue short shorts and a silver bikini top. The matching blue shirt she had tied around her waist hardly provided any additional coverage. To say she was decked out in our school colors would be an overstatement. Scantily clad in them would be more accurate. But, just in case you missed her, she was holding a huge, professionally rendered sign above her head. She looked kind of like a ring girl from a boxing match. You know, the ones who hold up the signs announcing what number the round is. But instead of a number, the sign read GO, DREW! YOU CAN DO IT!!!

I suspected that the same sign shop made it that had been responsible for the ON ANGLE'S WINGS banner.

"What is she doing?" Sam asked. "Hope is so not going to be threatened by that. Look at Drew. He's totally embarrassed." His red face was evident all the way across the soccer field.

"This is what happens when you work with amateurs," I said. "Come on, let's do damage control."

We had to weave our way through the kidlings who were all gaping, openmouthed, at Alexis's display. Even though she was wearing more than they'd normally see on the beach, there was something out of place about it on a soccer field teeming with children.

"I can't believe I'm pseudo-related to *that*," Hope said when we reached her. Alexis was spreading herself out on the first row of the bleachers, leaning back to collect some rays and show off her emaciated body while she waited for the game to begin.

"I just can't believe she'd so blatantly make a move on him right after you broke up," Sam added. "You'd think she'd at least wait until you'd left town for the summer."

"Yeah, she's good," I said.

"Good?" Hope scoffed. "Are you out of your skull? Drew's not going to fall for that crap."

"Well, it's not like he's ever had a cheering section before," I said. "I mean you hardly ever look up from your journal during a game."

"That's because he hardly ever has field time," Hope said.

"All I'm saying is that Alexis is making a big deal out of supporting him. Any guy would like that."

Sam nodded her head gravely, like she was agreeing with me. Okay, I admit we were being a bit cruel, but we needed to get things moving along. Hope was heading to New York in four days.

Drew was totally helping us out by playing into the act. Even though he was clearly embarrassed, Drew couldn't take his eyes off Alexis. Neither could the rest of the soccer team. *Both* soccer teams.

Coach Zach apparently realized what a distraction she was going to be during the game. He hurried over to Alexis and convinced her to cover up with the shirt she had tied around her waist. She agreed quite willingly. I assume because she didn't want to create a scene.

Riiight.

Once Alexis was looking a little more demure, Coach Zach sounded the air horn announcing that the scrimmage was set to start in a few minutes. As the kidlings scrambled for seats in the middle of the bleachers, my friends and I casually strolled over to the place on the end that had somehow become our usual spot. Hope clearly wanted to move us closer to Alexis, but there was no way to discreetly do that so she settled in beside us. Her eyes hardly left her stepsister the entire time. Even when David Beckham took the field—to the screams and adoration of the crowd and paparazzi.

The scrimmage began with both Eric and Drew in the game. That wasn't unusual for Eric since he was a starter, but Drew didn't usually get any play until we were up by a few points. Speaking of unusual, Hope was oddly vocal from the opening kickoff . . . or whatever you call it in soccer.

Sam, on the other hand . . .

Her eyes were closed and her lips were silently moving. "What are you doing?" I asked.

"Running lines," Sam said.

"But your boyfriend's playing," I reminded her.

"It's just a scrimmage. He'd understand."

"Yeah, but—"

"Where's Holly?" Sam suddenly asked. Her back went stiff as she eyed the crowd.

"What?"

"Holly?" she said. "I just realized . . . I haven't seen her all day."

"Belinda and Gary are missing too," Hope added. "I haven't seen that twig since I left the house."

"Unbelievable!" Sam said. "They're rehearsing. They snuck away for stage time. She was specifically told that we were expected to help out here. I hate how everybody at this freakin' school thinks they are exempt from the rules."

I weighed our options. It was kind of a dumb rule that we were all expected to watch a game that wasn't even part of the regular season when we had a huge audition on Friday. (Well, Blackstone had made it clear that as far as he was concerned, *I* wasn't auditioning for anything, but that's not the point.) Either we could stay at the game and continue our Hope and Drew manipulation or we could go off and rehearse too.

Like there was a choice.

"Let's get Jason and go," I suggested. Our scenemate was sitting on the other side of the bleachers with some of his friends who were neither soccer players nor Drama Geeks. (I know. There are a few of them at our school. The non-joiners.) Jason looked like he was into the game, but I was pretty sure a rehearsal would take precedence.

"No," Sam said. "I don't want to leave Eric's game."

"But you have no problem watching it with your eyes closed?" I asked.

"It's a matter of degrees."

"We can always rehearse after," Hope suggested.

"I promised Mom I'd go home and help her study," Sam said. "She's got a big test tomorrow and she's freaking out about it."

"Your mom is freaking out about a test?" Hope asked.

"That I'd like to . . . uh-oh." My eyes were diverted to the field. "Drew's getting pulled."

"Why? What happened?" Hope asked.

I shrugged. I hadn't been paying attention. I suspect it wasn't something good, since Drew had to pick himself up off the ground before he could leave the field. Alexis didn't even give him a chance to sit. She was on him as soon as he reached the bench.

"Unbelievable!" Hope said, though I personally thought it was not only believable, but expected.

"Why are you so bugged?" Sam asked.

"Are you kidding?" Hope asked. "How would you feel if Holly made a move on Eric?"

"But you broke up," I reminded her. "Technically, Drew is fair game."

"Doesn't mean I want to see him with that she-devil," Hope said. "Look at her! She's touching him!"

"Well, his hair was hanging down in his eyes," I said. "Did you expect him to brush it away himself?"

"He should be watching the game," Hope said.

No sooner had she said it than her words were proven true. A St. James player gave the ball a killer kick that sent it sailing over the field toward the benches. The crowd roared in warning as the ball continued its deadly arc, smashing into the back of Drew's head, and sending him crashing to his knees.

Alexis was stunned, as he, quite literally, fell at her feet.

Hope was up in a shot, rushing to his side. Sam and I shared an excited, though concerned, glance as we followed. That Hope had reacted so quickly was a good sign. That Drew had fallen so hard, was not. The crowd was up on its feet checking to see that he was okay.

Coach Zach was already down beside Drew as we reached them. "How many fingers?" he asked.

"Two and a half?" Drew guessed as his eyes focused on the coach's hand.

Coach Zach didn't like that answer. "Drew!"

"Well, did you want me to count your thumb?" Drew asked. "Technically, it's not a finger. It's a thumb."

"He's okay," Coach Zach announced to the gathering crowd. "A smartass, but okay."

Hope, Sam, and I each let out a sigh. We were all so concerned about Drew that it took a moment for us to realize we were only inches away from David Beckham. Well, Alexis had noticed. She was already making goo-goo eyes at him, forgetting all about Drew.

"Unbelievable," Hope said again, which brought Alexis back into reality.

"Oh, you're okay," she said, holding out a hand to help Drew up.

"Step off, hose-beast," Hope warned with a growl, actually scaring Alexis enough that she did back away. Hope held out her own hand for Drew. "Come on. We're going to put some ice on that."

"I'm okay," Drew insisted as he took her hand and stood up.

"I said we're putting ice on it," Hope said. "Now!"

"Okay," Drew agreed.

Game play resumed as Hope and Drew headed for the main campus. It was the last Sam and I saw of them for the day.

I Love You, You're Perfect, Now Change

"And how are my two best friends in the world on this fine and dandy summer morning?" Hope asked as she met Sam and me outside of Anne's classroom Thursday morning.

"Oh, dear, she's finally snapped," I said. We were all prepared to hunker down and work our scene to death all day. Mr. Randall had told everyone not to even bother checking in at the auditorium so we could get right to work. We weren't going to have enough time to psychoanalyze Hope of Sunnybrook Farm. No matter how much fun that could've been.

"Just happy is all," Hope said. "Alexis has lost her car privileges for the next month."

"How'd that happen?" Sam asked.

"She was caught with my private journal in her bedroom. She'd already been warned twice this year about stealing my stuff."

"You don't seem too broken up over the invasion of privacy," Sam said.

"It wasn't my *real* journal," Hope said, fingering the flash drive around her neck that held her most intimate writing. "It was *The Book of the Dead Puppy Poetry, Volume Six*. And I wouldn't say that Alexis *stole* it as much as I may have accidentally *left* it under her pillow after I got home from Drew's last night."

Sam and I looked at each other with raised eyebrows. We were both glad to hear that her mood had something to do with Drew. I noticed that her clothes had a more playful Goth-Ick look to them. She was wearing a black tank top with a flowing black skirt and a rainbow-striped scarf tied around her waist like a belt. Even her contacts were a cheerful shade of blue.

"You were at Drew's last night?" I asked.

"Getting back together?" Sam asked.

Hope recoiled at the suggestion. "Hell, no! We were . . . finding closure."

"Closure?" I asked with a smirk.

"Laugh at my vocabulary if you want," Hope said. "But we needed it. After we left the game, we got to talking and it all sort of came out. Everything we weren't dealing with since our fight. We are much better now. Dare I say, I think we can even be friends."

I *hate it* when all the good stuff happens offstage. "Congratulations," I said.

Sam didn't seem as ready as I was to accept defeat, though. "But your fight?"

"Was stupid," Hope said. "And not really about what we were fighting over. It doesn't matter. We've moved on."

"But you and Drew—"

"Work better as friends," she insisted.

"But—"

"Let it go, Sam," Hope said. "You're taking this harder than I am. Come on, we've got work to do."

Hope started setting up the room for our scene, forcing us to join in or look like slackers while she did all the work. Sam clearly wanted to discuss the great Hope and Drew friendship pact further, but Hope had shut down the line of inquiry. I wasn't all that broken up over it either. I found myself surprisingly happy to hear that Hope and Drew were moving on.

When Jason joined in a few minutes later, the subject was effectively dropped for good. We had some serious rehearsing to do.

"Okay, let's try this again," Jason said as he hit play on the nature sounds machine.

I'd like to say that the day off had helped us clear our heads. And that Hope's improved mood had added to the performance. But while Hope was markedly more into the scene than she'd been the other day, the group was still floundering. Jason and Sam were still under- and overplaying moments. Hope was bringing too much broad comedy to the role. And I was still dropping lines . . . among other problems.

We all knew it wasn't working, but none of us could make it right.

No matter how many times we ran through it, the thing just didn't *feel* good.

Actually, it felt like crap.

"I need a break," Sam said as we entered the second hour of rehearsals. "I'm going to get some drinks from the pavilion." She looked at me. "Come."

"Yes, ma'am."

As soon as the door was safely closed behind us, Sam said, "I don't think it's over."

"Of course not," I said. "We've still got the rest of the day to rehearse. It'll come together."

"Not the scene," she said. "Though that's been pretty crappy. I meant Hope and Drew. She did a one eighty on her mood too fast."

"She says she found closure," I reminded Sam.

"Please. They're destined to be together."

"Or," I said, "they've been dating for years and have known each other most of their lives. It's only natural that they continue the friendship."

"Don't quash my buzz," she said, rubbing her hands together. "I feel like our plans are coming to fruition."

"Mwa-ha," I said. "Ha."

"We just need to come up with a new phase," she said. "I think the Alexis thing has run its course."

"Sam, it's over," I said as we reached the pavilion. "Why are you obsessing?"

"Because Hope's our friend," Sam said. "Don't you want her to be happy?"

I grabbed a couple drinks out of the refrigerator and handed them to Sam, then grabbed a couple for me to take. "Does this have something to do with Eric?"

"What?" Sam asked. "Why?"

I'd caught her totally off guard by the question. Have to say, I was a bit surprised by it myself. I hadn't made the connection until that moment. "He's going away," I explained. "For the rest of the summer."

"But if I get into Blackstone's program, I'll be a train ride away," she reminded me.

I didn't want to ask the question, but I had to. "And if you don't?"

"If I don't?" she asked like it was the first time she'd considered the possibility. "Then, I'm still here and he's gone."

"Have you guys talked about that?"

"We've been more focused on me getting into Blackstone's program."

"So that would be a no."

Sam played with the cap on one of the bottles, nervously twisting it off and on. "I don't know where things stand with us," she finally said. "We've only been going out a little over a month. Are we exclusive? Will we see other people while he's away? Will we agree to be exclusive while he secretly dates other girls that I won't know about because he's three thousand miles away?"

"Since Drew and Eric are best friends," I said, reasoning it out, "and if Drew's still going out with Hope while she's away in New York, I'm guessing part of you thinks that will be an example to Eric that he should stay true to you while he's gone as well."

"Wow," she said. "That makes me sound stupid, selfish, *and* insecure. Impressive."

"No," I insisted. "You're not any of those things. Well, maybe insecure. But that's a normal relationship thing. Happens all the time on TV." Since I don't have any actual relationship experience myself, I've got to go with what I know. "Tell Eric you want to be exclusive. I haven't seen him with anyone else since you two started going out. He'll be fine with it."

"I can't bring it up," she said. "He's got to bring it up. Otherwise I look desperate."

"You'd rather look insane by forcing Hope and Drew back together?"

"Please stop making logical arguments," she said. "It makes it so much harder to ignore reality."

"So, you'll talk to him?" I asked.

"One thing at a time," she said. "Let's see if we can get me in this acting program, then I won't have to deal with it."

"I guess ignoring your issues is kind of a way to deal with them."

"Always," she said.

We switched to a lighter subject for the walk back to Anne's classroom. I suggested she consider releasing an album for younger kids titled *Off to Pee I Go* and that got us started on a whole slew of inspirational bathroom songs for infants learning to potty train. We were laughing quite freely by the time we returned to Anne's classroom with drinks for every-body.

The laughing stopped when Hope announced, "Mr. Randall says we're up for some stage time."

We should have been happy to get the chance to rehearse in front of our teacher onstage, but that didn't seem to be the consensus. We weren't ready to show anyone what we had. Whatever *that* was. I think we were all a little embarrassed when we entered the empty auditorium and saw him sitting alone in the front row.

During the school year, Mr. Randall usually leaves us on our own to work on scenes. I guess he realized how much was at stake so he was sitting in with all the groups to watch a run-through and then give his advice. Notice I didn't use the word "critique" there. Yeah. I've come to realize that our favorite teacher never critiques us, so much as tells us what we're doing well and what we could do better. Rarely does he ever tell us when we're doing something wrong—aside from not speaking loudly enough or dropping a few pages of text.

I don't think I was the only one that wasn't ready to start up again. Even with our short break, we were all exhausted, both emotionally and physically from the earlier rehearsals. But we would try to do our best for him, considering.

With little fanfare, we got up onstage and performed the scene for our teacher, just as we had dozens of times before in class over the years. The only difference was we weren't waiting for a grade from him. What was ultimately at stake was much more important than that. At least it was for Sam and Jason. And maybe even Hope. There was still a chance she could dazzle Blackstone in spite of his attitude toward character actors. I was pretty sure that I was far out of consideration.

But I don't think any of us would have been helped by the performance we'd just given.

"I see Mr. Blackstone's criticism got to you guys as well," Mr. Randall said with a sigh in his voice. "I had hoped if anyone would be immune . . ."

It would be what? His prize pupils? His star students? He certainly hadn't stuck up for us much during the critiques. I knew I was being unfair, but that's what I was thinking at the time.

Hope, on the other hand, spoke her mind.

"It would be who?" she asked. "Us? And why is that? Because I'm *dying* to hear from another person who thinks I can only play character parts! Glinda the Good Witch, my ass!"

There was a long silence in the auditorium. For Hope to have an outburst like that was certainly not unusual. For her to direct it at a teacher, on the other hand . . .

"I'm sorry," she finally said.

Mr. Randall was looking at us in that way that you can clearly tell he was trying to figure out what to say. Or, more specifically, *how* to say it. We get that look from the teachers a lot around school. They have a tendency to fear honesty with the students since any one of us could probably get them fired in between calls to the stylist and the therapist.

"I know Mr. Blackstone's criticisms were harsh," he said. "But, let's be honest, you're all going to hear much worse outside of Orion. This school is set up to be a safe environment for the students. Sometimes, it may be too safe. I'm not saying I agree with everything that Mr. Blackstone said, but I think you all needed to hear it. If only to learn how to accept criticism. So far, no one has dealt all that well. Instead of rallying, you've completely fallen apart. I have to admit, I expected more from you guys."

He let that sink in for a moment.

"So, enough of the teen angst?" I said.

"More than," Mr. Randall agreed.

"We'll work on it," Jason added. Hope was nodding in agreement.

"I can give you the stage for another half hour," Mr. Randall said, getting up. "I suggest you make good use of your time."

"We will," Sam promised as we watched our teacher go.

If only we had a clue where to begin.

Into the Woods

I guess we were all thinking about the best way to proceed because there was a lot of quiet going on in the auditorium. I could feel our half hour slipping away as we stood in silence, like we were in the play *Act Without Words*. (*Aside:* Which is pretty much what the title indicates.)

Jason was the first to speak.

"This can work," he burst out with a kind of frenetic excitement as he moved about the stage. "All we need to do is make some choices . . . give it some direction. We've all been too afraid to do what we know we have to do."

"Where did he come from?" I asked.

"I guess he's found his muse," Hope said. "And she is on speed."

Apparently she was on speed and had a death wish, because Jason turned to Sam and said, "Maybe you can take it down . . . just a notch. At the point where you're calling Hope a puppet. I think the scene was starting to get away from us there."

"And maybe you can pick it up a bit," Sam said. "You kind of mumbled through the opening line. It didn't give me much to work with."

Jason stopped. "I don't *mumble*."

"No," Sam backtracked. "I just meant that you've got to—"

"Get past the first row?" Jason asked, echoing Blackstone's critique of him.

"I didn't . . . I was just saying—"

"Speaking of getting past the first row, what was with that pause you took?" Jason asked.

"What pause?" Sam asked back. I knew exactly what pause Jason was talking about. In the middle of the scene, there was a moment of silence that was kind of . . . prolonged.

"The one that lasted five minutes," he said.

Okay, maybe not *that* long. But not all that short either.

"Very funny," she said. "I was working through some internal . . ." Her face fell. I think she realized that what Blackstone had said to her was right. Sometimes, she takes moments that are so small, the audience doesn't know what's going on.

If we kept this up, it was bound to spiral out of control. "Look," I jumped in. "Let's move past the moments. We have to consider the entire scene. I don't think it's working. Maybe we should choose a different one."

"Like what?" Hope said.

Trouble was, I didn't have any suggestions. All I knew was

that something was wrong with this scene. I had no clue what alternate one could work for us.

"I think you'd make a great Puck," Sam suggested.

Hope spun on her. "Meaning what?" she asked, like there was any doubt. Puck was the trickster, the fool. Depending on how you played him (or her, if you want), she/he could be very big with the broad comedy, which *was* Hope's specialty.

"She just means we might want to go with a scene that plays to your strengths," Jason said. "To all of our strengths, I mean."

Hope filled in the blanks. "No. You mean you want me to be the comic relief."

I was still going for peacekeeper. "You do usually—"

"And what if I want to stretch a bit?" Hope asked with no regard for the peace whatsoever. "Try something new? I'm getting a little tired of everyone just assuming Sam and Holly are the only ones up for the girl's spot in Blackstone's program. I have as much of a chance of impressing him as anyone."

I went with my calm voice. "I don't think anyone—"

"Oh, please," Hope said. "Sam and Jason have been going around all week like we're holding them back. Why do you think they blocked the entire scene while you were out on Monday? Did they even give you a chance to contribute to the blocking?"

"Hope!" Sam said. "That's not fair."

"No, it's not," Hope said. "But it's obvious—"

"Obvious?" Jason jumped in. "You want to talk obvious? Let's talk about your larger-than-life choices."

"Guys, we don't have time for this," Sam reminded them. "We have to get some work done. I'm not about to lose my shot at this program 'cause you guys can't get it together."

"See what I mean," Hope said. *"Her* shot. Like it's a guarantee."

It was one thing to exhibit this kind of naked backstabbing aggression when Holly Mayflower was around. It was another thing entirely when friends started turning on one another, as Sam, Hope, and Jason had all quite literally managed to do. Me? I was in the center of the three of them, looking at those backs that had turned.

And don't think it was lost on me that none of them were criticizing my performance. I guess Blackstone really had said it all last week.

"This is stupid," I said. Mr. Randall would be so disappointed to see that this is how we'd reacted to his pep talk. "We're not going to get anywhere in our scene if we don't work together."

"Now, there's the best idea I've heard all morning," Hope said.

I had no clue what she was talking about. "Hope?"

"I'm done working together," she said as she stormed off the stage and out of the theater.

The rest of us stood in silence for a moment. "Humph," I finally said to Sam. "You were the one who wanted her to be the old Hope. Personally, I think we would have gotten further with her when she was morbid and depressed."

"Is this funny to you?" Jason asked. "Just because you don't have a shot at Blackstone's program doesn't mean you shouldn't take this seriously. I thought you actually cared about your friend over there."

Usually, my attempts at humor are better received. "What are you talking about?"

"Never mind," Jason said, before taking a page out of Hope's book and storming off, stage right.

"What the hell was that?" I asked, but I got no response from Sam.

I get that the pressure had been building. We'd all been tip-toeing around these issues like cats on a hot tin roof all week. But for that explosion . . . well, it was just so unnecessary.

And Sam was still disturbingly quiet.

"Do you know what he was talking about?" I asked. "About me not caring for you?"

"No," Sam said in the least reassuring tone ever.

"Sam."

"He doesn't think you're taking this seriously when you make jokes like that," Sam said.

"Yeah, but that's what we do," I reminded her. "We make jokes. It's how we deal."

"Some people don't like jokes all the time," Sam said. "Sometimes the stress doesn't let people see the funny."

"You don't need to stress," I said. "You know you're good. I'm the one that got ripped to shreds by the country's fore-most authority on acting, remember?"

"And just because Blackstone said some nice things about me, I don't have anything to worry about?" Sam asked. "Don't you get it? You have options. You can do whatever you want when you get out of here. Go to whatever school you get into. Orion is it for me. I spent my grandparents' money on this place. I have to do everything in my power to make sure I get a full scholarship if I want to go to college. Do you know what kind of help getting into Blackstone's program would be for me? So I'm sorry if I don't feel like joking right now. I have too much riding on this scene."

Suddenly, I didn't feel like joking either. There had been something nagging at the back of my mind for the past week and a half. Something that I needed the answer to. And I needed it right now. "If we weren't best friends, would you have agreed to do this scene with me?"

"What?"

"You heard me," I said.

"Don't be an idiot."

"I'm not an idiot. I want to know. With so much riding on this for you, would you have chosen me to be in the scene?"

"Blackstone—"

"I'm not asking about Blackstone," I said. "I'm asking about you. When you made that joke the other day about me sucking as an actor . . . did you mean it?"

"Well . . . I wouldn't say you *sucked*."

A ten-ton truck slammed into me, right there, center stage. My entire body felt like it had collapsed, but somehow I managed to stay on my feet, while Sam realized what she had just said.

"Bryan. Oh, God! I'm sorry. I didn't mean—"

She moved toward me, but I pushed her away.

I didn't say anything. I calmly collected my things and made my way up the aisle. Then, once I was sure that Sam was not watching . . . I ran.

Out of Hall Hall and into the halls of Orion Academy.

My fleeing footsteps echoed through the empty halls as I passed classroom after classroom. I veered to the right when I heard the soccer team in the pavilion. Figures they'd break for lunch early the one time I was looking for someplace to be alone.

I burst out the doors and headed for the parking lot. Electra was waiting for me, but I couldn't get in. I was in no condition to drive the winding Malibu roads. The last thing I needed was to hit a corner too hard, roll off a cliff, and land in a gully below.

I wasn't ready to be found. I had to go somewhere Sam would never in a bajillion years think to look for me. If she even bothered to look for me, that is.

I ran for the trees. Following the well-worn path, I was heading for the one place I knew I could be alone: the soccer field. With the team munching away, I had at least a good hour to be by myself. That would give me more than enough time to calm down so I could drive safely out of there.

I twisted my way through the trees. The promised land opened up before me. Never in my life had I been so happy to see a sporting field of any kind, much less the one sport that had become the bane of my existence.

I was home free.

Until I nearly ran right into Drew at the edge of the tree line.

Beyond Therapy

There was a moment of confused hesitation. Like we had both been caught doing something we weren't supposed to be doing.

"What are you doing here?" he asked.

"What are *you* doing here?" I asked back, hoping that my eyes weren't all wet from the tears that I was trying to hold back.

"I needed to get the ball," he said, holding up his soccer ball.

"Noooo," I said with a little more childlike petulance than I intended. But he *had* invaded my private spot. Not that it had ever been my private spot before. Not that he didn't have more right to be there than I did, considering he was the soccer player and I was the . . . well, I wasn't sure what I was anymore. I used to think of myself as an actor-photographer. Now I wasn't even a hyphen.

"What are you doing *here?*" I asked. "The rest of the team's at lunch."

"I wanted to get in some more practice." He walked to the center of the field bouncing the soccer ball off his knee as he went.

Great. I was having a total breakdown, and Drew chose this time to be all gung ho about his game. Why couldn't he just be a quitter like Alexis? Leave it to Drew to show a commitment to something he loved. I *so* did not need that at the moment, so I turned and walked away.

"Why are you leaving?" he asked.

Like there was an easy answer to *that* question. As such, I deflected it. "I think we're still in that period where as Hope's friend I'm supposed to hate you."

"You've hated me for years. Why should today be any different?"

"I never hated you. I just don't like you. There's a difference. Hating is more active."

"And you haven't done anything active in years."

"Exactly."

"Well, why don't you try something active for a change? I could use a goalie."

I looked over at the big net he was facing. Was he actually suggesting that I, Bryan Stark, engage in physical activity? "You're kidding, right?"

"It's not much of a challenge to kick the ball into an open net."

"And you think I'd be more of a challenge than empty

space?" I asked. With my life falling apart around me, self-deprecating wasn't that hard.

"You're not *that* bad," Drew said.

"I think Coach Zach would disagree," I said. "I did nearly maim him in gym class last year."

"Okay, baseball was never your sport," he said. "But you used to be pretty good at soccer. You were one of the top guys at soccer camp."

"In fifth grade!"

"Bryan," he said. "I could really use the help."

When someone who you can hardly have a civil conversation with lays himself bare before you (not *that* way) and asks for your help, how can you say no?

"No," I said.

"Bryan!"

"Okay. Fine." I took position in front of the net. I still had my own issues to work through, but maybe some strenuous exercise would help me put things in perspective. Little did I know there wouldn't be all that much exercise. Drew's first shot at the net went wide and missed the huge target by a good five feet. We both watched as it rolled off into the woods behind me. It came to a stop at the foot of an oak tree.

After about ten seconds with neither of us moving, Drew yelled, "Go get it!"

"*You* kicked it!"

"Bryan!"

"Okay. Fine," I said, again. Since I was closer, I guess he did have a point.

I went back and retrieved the ball, then threw it out to him and took position back in the net. The next shot came directly toward me, but I missed it. Score one for Drew. I spent the next few minutes blocking—or attempting to block—goals. I don't know if I was really good or if Drew was that bad, but I made more grabs than I would have expected.

Neither of us spoke while we played, which was nice. It gave me time to think. But I wasn't exactly thinking about what Blackstone or Sam had said. I was thinking about Drew. I know. Weird. But it was kind of related to what I was going through. Drew had been playing soccer for about as long as I had been doing theater. And if this practice was any indication, his abilities with a soccer ball were about on par with my stage work. I mean, really, I shouldn't have been stopping that many goals.

After a while, I started to work up a sweat, which I don't really like to do. When the ball sailed past the net another time, I yelled, "Time!" and took a seat on the field. Drew was clearly annoyed with me for stopping, but didn't say anything about it. He ran to retrieve the ball and joined me on the grass beneath the net.

"Thanks," he said as he sat. "I really need the work."

"I can see that," I joked.

The silence that he responded with told me I had touched a nerve.

We sat in that silence for a while longer, before I finally said what I had been thinking.

"How do you do it?" I asked.

"Do what?"

"This." I waved my hand out over the soccer field. "Your best friend is David Beckham in training and you're"—I looked into his gray eyes and faltered—"not."

"Thanks," he said, tugging at the blades of grass around him. "Sorry I made you exercise. I didn't know you'd be all insulting about it."

This was not going the way I had intended. "No. I'm not trying to be mean. I'm just . . ." I paused to gather my thoughts. "I was at Mom's store the other day and I stumbled across that picture you painted for her. You remember the one? That you gave her for the grand opening?"

"How can I forget?" he said. "She had it hanging over the register for two years. How embarrassing."

Just wait till he saw it in the store window.

"You're an incredibly talented artist," I said. "Amazing. But you're not doing it anymore. Instead, you're focused on soccer. Do you really think you're going to be a professional soccer player when you get out of school?"

"You really thought I was amazing?"

"Drew. Focus."

"Okay," he said. "Well, what about you? Do you really think you're going to be a professional actor when you get out of here?"

Leave it to Drew to hit the head on the nail with the first try. "Apparently not," I said.

The silence returned.

This time, Drew was the one to break it. "I heard about

what that guy said. Blackstone?" Thank you, Alexis. I swear that girl gets more hits than Perez Hilton. And she doesn't even have a MySpace page. She gossips the old-fashioned way: person to person.

If he pulled that "it's just one man's opinion" crap, I think it was entirely possible that I would lead him through the trees and push him off the bluff.

But Drew was much more eloquent than that.

"That sucks."

"Succinct, yet accurate."

"But was it that big of a surprise?"

My eyes bugged out. I started searching for the quickest route to the bluff.

"No," he quickly added. "Listen. It's like you asked me about being a professional soccer player. I know there's a slim chance." I gave him a look. "Okay. It's never going to happen. But that doesn't stop me from enjoying the game. Did you really think you were that good? Is this a total shock to hear?"

"I knew I wasn't as good as Sam," I said. Apparently, Sam knew it too . . . and more.

"Maybe you're so upset because you kind of believe what Blackstone said?"

"Oh, God!" I burst into tears. I didn't care about how it looked. Drew had seen me cry before. My grandfather's funeral a few years back had some real good crying going on.

That didn't mean Drew was comfortable with it. "Oh. Okay. I wasn't prepared for that."

"Why not?" I asked through the free-flowing tears. "You know how much acting means to me."

"Really?" he asked. "Acting?"

"Hello! Have you met me?"

"If you had said how important 'theater' was to you . . . that I'd get. You've loved theater since forever. But the acting part? I don't know. It never seemed all that big a deal."

"What does that even mean?"

"It's like me and soccer," he said. "I like being part of a team. I enjoy the cheers of the crowd. And, you have to admit, I look damn good in my soccer uniform." I gave no reaction to this comment. "But when it comes down to the actual playing . . ."

"Yeah, but—"

"Don't you theater people have some kind of saying like, 'Those who can, act. Those who can't, direct'?"

"That's an insult," I explained. "A joke."

"It makes sense to me. You're a good photographer. So, obviously you've got an eye for setting a scene. And you're always telling people what to do."

"I don't tell—" You know what? I didn't even bother to finish the sentence. Neither of us would have believed it, anyway. "But acting—"

"Is the only thing you've tried in theater," he said. "So what? You can't act. There are like a hundred other jobs you can do. For me it's play soccer or coach. And I'm not a sidelines kind of guy. So what are you whining about?"

I wouldn't say that I was *whining*. I prefer "introspective complaining." But he did have a point. Maybe I'm not an actor.

There are other things I can do. And director-photographer does have a nice flow to it.

Imagine that. With one simple phrase, Drew had totally lifted my mood and solved my entire identity crisis.

Okay, that was a lie. I was still miserable. But I wasn't quite as miserable as I'd been when I got there. I needed some time to myself.

And maybe to hatch a scheme.

"Thanks," I said getting up. "I still think you should get back into art, though. You can do that along with soccer, you know."

"We'll see," he said. "You up for some more practice?"

"Not really," I said.

"I get that," Drew said. "Later."

"Later," I said as I walked away.

Now that I was considerably calmer, I got in Electra and drove cautiously out of the parking lot. I'd considered going back to the theater to talk to Sam, but I wasn't ready yet. And I'm not all that sure she was ready to talk to me either.

It wasn't like I was abandoning my team by leaving. They'd already abandoned me. Both Hope's and Jason's cars were gone from the parking lot before I got to Electra. They may have given up, but I hadn't. The scheme forming in my mind was already going full force. I just needed to get home to work it out.

Before Dawn

Canoodle was bouncing all over the kitchen before I even walked through the door. You can imagine how she greeted me once I was inside. I gave her a rub behind the ear, and a brief bit of attention, but pushed past her before she was ready to let me go. I was on a mission. I didn't even stop for a snack, which is highly unusual for me.

I ran to my room and grabbed my copy of *The Riverside Shakespeare*. It wasn't as big as the book that Jason had brought to school earlier, but it was still a rather large tome, and one of the definitive collection of old Willie's works. To get me in the mood, I loaded the soundtrack to Baz Luhrmann's version of *Romeo + Juliet* into my CD player and began to brush up on my Shakespeare.

Our scene wasn't working. That much was painfully clear. Not just because we were all still reeling from Blackstone's critiques—though that *was* something we were going to have to deal with. No. It was because it was the wrong scene for our talents. (Or my friends' talents. I, apparently, didn't have any.) The only way we were going to have a chance with Blackstone was to choose a different scene. And to do that, I had to begin by considering the strengths of my team.

Hope needed comedy, but she wanted drama. That was going to take some doing.

Jason was a great actor, but broad comedy was not his strength. He was better with more straightforward roles.

Sam was absolutely amazing and could perform almost any role. The problem would be convincing her of that. And finding that perfect role for her to perform.

I scanned down the table of contents. The tragedies were too heavy to learn in one night. The histories, as one might suspect, had too much history involved. Blackstone could very well decide it would be fun to throw in a little quiz after we finished our scene. No. We'd have to stick to comedy,

Starting with our chosen selection, *A Midsummer Night's Dream*, I quickly flipped through the pages of the play. I wasn't reading every page, just checking to see what characters were in which scenes. When I came to a scene with four parts, I grabbed a Post-it note off my desk and bookmarked the page. Once I'd gone through the entire play, I went back and skimmed the scenes so I could get a quick read on what they were about.

A Midsummer's Night Dream didn't work. None of the scenes matched our talents or our needs. I immediately moved on to *Twelfth Night*. Jason had said something about scenes where one of us wouldn't have much to do. That was one of my goals. Now, I just had to meet the other criteria.

I found a scene toward the end of the play that was even more perfect than I had imagined. Technically it was a five-person scene, but that didn't matter. It would work beautifully.

I ran down to my mom's studio and fired up her copier, making several duplicates of the pages: one for each of my scenemates and a few for me to work on myself. Once that was done, I went back to my room and got to work.

I started by looking up the play online and learning all that I could in the time I had. Even though we had examined *Twelfth Night* back in sophomore year, I didn't have automatic recall on these things, so I needed to refamiliarize myself with the text. The play is about an identical twin brother and sister (scientifically impossible, I know) who each think the other is dead when they wash up on the shores of a distant land. The comedy comes from the people who keep confusing them for each other, even though one is male and the other is, obviously, female. The scene I chose was the revelation at the end where their identities come to light and the day is ultimately saved.

Once I understood the scene, I tore it apart and put it back together. I made notes in the margins, wrote in questions for myself, and cut the scene to shreds, marking out the beats, units, and all those other things we'd learned during script analysis classes. Then I grabbed a clean copy of the scene and wrote down my ideas for the blocking. If we were going to do what I had in mind, we were going to have to stage the scene perfectly.

All this work took way longer than I'd expected. It was almost time for Mom to be home. Normally, I would have waited for her before I headed out, but we didn't have a moment to waste. I grabbed my cell phone and made for the back door.

I hit Hope's name on the speed dial as I reached the kitchen. Canoodle came bounding up to me as it rang. I gave our four-legged guest more some attention as Hope came on the line.

"Hello?"

"It's me."

"About frakking time," she said. "We've been calling all afternoon."

Oops. I guess I was so into my work, I hadn't noticed the phone vibrating when they called. Or the messages on it either.

"Sorry, I was . . . involved," I said, pulling myself away from Canoodle so I could write Mom a note. "You haven't talked to Sam, have you?"

"I'm with her right now," Hope said. "She called me when she couldn't reach you. Did you forget you were her ride home today?"

Oops, again. I'd have to apologize when I saw her. Actually, I think we all had some apologizing to do.

"And Jason?" I asked.

"He's on his way over," Hope said. "We really need to get in some serious rehearsing."

"Just what I had in mind," I said as Canoodle barked to

remind me that she was in the room. "I'll be right there." As she rubbed against my leg, inspiration struck again. "Wait. No. Better idea. Meet me at school."

"School's closed," she said.

"Just meet me there," I said. "And pick up a pizza on the way. I'm starving." I hung up the phone before she could respond. It was rude to cut the conversation short like that, but Hope would never have let me go otherwise.

Oh, and I would have gotten the pizza on my own, but I had another stop to make.

I gave Canoodle another good rub behind the ears to thank her for being there. Then, I grabbed a set of emergency keys from the drawer beside the sink and made my way out to Electra, and, ultimately, to the headmaster's house.

My detour took a bit longer than I'd expected, but I still made it to school before the rest of my group. The sun was already dipping toward the ocean as Hope pulled up in the pink-and-purple nightmare on wheels. It was quite entertaining watching Jason unfold himself out of the backseat. I had yet to ride in the matchbox car. Seeing Jason, who was about my height, struggling to get out told me that I wouldn't be hopping in any time soon.

As we gathered by the school entrance, there was a moment of awkwardness among us all, but mostly between Sam and me.

"I'm sorry," she said. "Of course I want you on my team. I will always want you on my team. I will always need you on my side."

As apologies go, that one was pretty good.

"No matter how bad I suck?" I asked. Leave it to me to spoil a nice moment.

"No matter how much you suck," she agreed.

"Good," I said. "Then, here." I handed them the pages I had printed out on the copier in Mom's studio. We could have spent another hour apologizing for the stupidity of the day, but we had for more pressing issues to deal with.

"What's this?" Jason asked.

"Our new scene," I said. "With some notes on blocking I marked down."

They all looked skeptical as they perused the pages from our *Twelfth Night* script.

Sam, the speed reader, was the first to notice the discrepancy. "This is a five-person scene," she said.

"It's okay," Jason said. "Antonio only has two lines. We can cut them or reassign them."

"No cutting," I said. "I'll be playing Antonio."

"That still leaves four other parts," Sam said.

"Not since you'll be playing both Viola and Sebastian," I said.

"You want me to play a girl and a guy?" Sam asked.

"The plot revolves around the fact that they're identical twins," I explained a fact that she already knew. "You can pull it off."

"And what about the rest of us?" Hope asked.

This was going to take some finessing. I was about to screw Hope over, but it had to be done.

"You're going to be Olivia," I said.

"I've only got a few lines," she said.

"Yes, but it's the kind of part you've been wanting to play," I reminded her. "She's a noblewoman."

"But. I've. Only. Got. A. Few. Lines."

It had finally happened. Hope and I were going to have a serious conversation.

"You know I adore you," I said. "And I know you can play any role that you set your mind to. But let's be honest. Blackstone has already made his decision. There's nothing you can do tomorrow to convince him of what I already know. This is going to come down to Sam and Jason versus Holly and Gary. We need to help them win."

I waited for a response. When she didn't say anything, I got in a final dig. "As Sam's best friends, don't we owe it to her to make sure she beats the crap out of Holly . . . figuratively speaking, of course."

"I have no problem with Sam literally beating the crap out of her," Hope said.

"So you're in?" I asked.

"I'm in," Hope said.

"Don't worry," I said. "You'll still get your moments."

"Oh, I know," she said.

I turned to Jason.

"I'm in too," he said.

I turned to Sam.

"I'm not so sure," Sam said, totally spoiling the momentum I was trying to build. "Don't get me wrong. I love that you guys are willing to do this for me. And, Bryan, I appreciate all the work you put in . . . but if I'm going to be both Viola and Sebastian in this scene, you've got me talking to myself. I can't pull that off."

"Yes," I said. "You can. You just have to trust me."

"I do trust you," Sam said. "But I'm not so sure I trust myself. We do this tomorrow."

"Would I let you look stupid?"

"Yes," Sam said, finally allowing herself to crack a smile and relieve some of the pressure. "Okay. But how are we supposed to block the scene when the stage is inside and we're locked out here?"

I looked at her with a raised eyebrow.

"We are *not* about to break into school," she said.

"Not at all," I replied, pulling a set of keys out of my pocket. "I have the keys."

I knew that watching the headmaster's dog would come in handy at some point. (Okay, well, I hadn't *known* it, but I had hoped.) After I filled my friends in on the detour I took through the headmaster's house to search for the keys to school on the way over, Hope grabbed the pizza out of the car and we slipped inside.

I've been at school before when there was no one left in the building. Being among the last out after a show or coming in on a Saturday for rehearsal is always fun. It's like we have the run of the place. But being there when we weren't supposed to be was a kind of rebellion that the four of us didn't normally take part in.

I guess Sam was right when she said the students at this school acted like the rules don't apply to them. And, for once, we were acting like our classmates.

After a quick dinner, we got to work breaking down the scene and discussing the situation. We read through the piece a couple times to get a feel for the words. As I suspected, Sam already had some of the lines down from when we read it sophomore year. (Told you she was a freak.)

Jason and Hope had a harder time committing their new lines to memory, but by midnight, they were doing pretty well. I made sure we spent enough time working on character and building our parts that the lines became second nature since we were focused on the meaning of what we were saying more than the actual words.

The late hour wasn't a problem since we had each used Hope's cell phone reception to call our parents and pull the old "I'm spending the night at a friend's house" routine. We were pretty sure none of our parents would follow up with each other, though Sam's mom is always an unknown element when it comes to parental responsibility. As for my mom, I guess she was just happy to hear I was hanging out with Jason. I do have an inordinate amount of female friends.

After midnight we went over the blocking. That was the real challenge.

"Told you I'd look like an idiot talking to myself," Sam said with no joy in her tone.

"That's because you're not committing to the shift," I said. "It has to be decisive. You break character. You become the new one. It has to be fast. And it has to be complete." I snapped my fingers. "Viola." And snapped again. "Sebastian." Snap. "Viola." Snap. "Sebastian."

Hope and Jason joined me as we snapped and chanted, "Viola. Sebastian. Viola. Sebastian . . ." while Sam shifted the physicality from one to the other with each snap. We did that until it became second nature for her. Then, we did it some more.

We helped facilitate the change in characters by pulling some set pieces out of storage for her to move between when changing from male to female. Crossing behind a pillar would serve visually as the transition. Add to that some good old-fashioned suspension of disbelief and we were halfway to our scene.

But the work wasn't done yet.

"No, Hope," I said gently. "You're too haughty. Olivia is prim and proper, but she's also vulnerable. She's worried about looking like a fool while at the same time she'd never permit anyone to play her for one. Got it?"

"I think."

"And Jason, you need to play to the house," I reminded him. "Tomorrow, choose a seat four or five rows behind Blackstone and play the scene to that seat. Imagine someone in that seat and keep reminding yourself that they need to see and hear everything you do and say. 'K?"

"Okay."

"All right," I said. "Let's try this again."

We ran through the scene once more, taking my latest notes into consideration. It was better, but not perfect. "Let's run it again," I said. "Oh, and does anyone have any suggestions for me?" I wasn't really worried about my performance because I only had a couple lines, but I didn't want my friends to think I was just being critical of them while I thought my performance was perfect.

And, wouldn't you know, they picked my two lines apart.

Actors!

By four o'clock we were all pretty tired. We camped out in the set storage room on some old couches and mattresses that parents had donated to the shows over the years. Those of us with cell phones set the alarms to make sure we woke with plenty of time to freshen up and get outside before we were found inside where we weren't supposed to be.

Hope found a daybed along the back wall of the storage room, and I curled up on a mattress on the floor beside her. Sam and Jason spread out on a pair of couches on the other side of the room. We probably could have pulled everything together, but we were all too exhausted. We pretty much collapsed where we were.

Maybe I was overtired, but my mind was racing so much with our scene that I couldn't shut it down to get some rest.

I wasn't the only one.

"Bryan," Hope whispered.

"Yeah," I whispered back. I couldn't hear Sam and Jason from where we were, but I didn't want to wake them if they had managed to nod off.

"In case things get too crazy tomorrow," she said. "Or, later today, I guess . . . I just wanted to say that I think we've got a great scene. You done good."

Wow. It was so unlike Hope to give a nice compliment like that. Not that she never had a kind word or anything, but her compliments were usually couched in a joke. No one could backhand a compliment like Hope Rivera.

"By the way," she said. "I should kill you for your little scheme to force me and Drew back together, but I'm in a forgiving mood lately. So just know that you're on probation, if you should ever think of doing something like that again . . ."

She let the end of that threat hang in the air. I should have known Hope wouldn't just compliment me for my stellar directing. I also should have expected that Hope would have been onto our scheme from the start.

Considering her "forgiving mood," I couldn't help but ask, "Any chance you'll let me read that monologue you wrote last week?"

"Nope," she replied, rolling over. "I shredded it."

I settled into sleep, secure in the knowledge that it was quite possible we'd never know exactly what it was that Hope and Drew had been fighting about. And, honestly, I didn't really mind.

Awake and Sing!

Morning came quickly, considering we didn't have much night left by the time I finally nodded off. I woke up before my alarm rang, staring at a different ceiling than I had been the rest of the week.

I was more nervous for this audition than any I'd ever had before. Even more than I'd been for the monologues last week. My fears weren't for myself. Blackstone had made it pretty clear that I was out of consideration. No. I was nervous for my friends. I wanted Hope to have her moment to shine. I wanted to see Jason move up to the next level in his acting. And I wanted Sam to do nothing less than give a performance that Blackstone would be raving about for years to come.

It was a lot to ask from one single scene, but we'd put in the work. Why not hope for the best?

Our cell phones started beeping in unison. We all reluctantly got up and made our way to the bathrooms to freshen up as sunlight filled the empty halls. We did the best we could with our clothes. Sam had a change of outfit in her mom's book closet, and Hope had a different shirt in her locker. Jason and I rifled through the ill-equipped costume closet for new shirts, but they all smelled old and musty so we just stuck with what we had worn the day before. I was sure people would notice, but there was very little we could do about it.

After grabbing breakfast from the vending machines, we locked up the school and sat in Electra to wait for someone to come by and open it up for us. It didn't take long. Not five minutes after we set up camp in the parking lot, Mr. Randall pulled up beside us.

"Looks like some people are ready to get a jump on the day," he said.

He had no idea.

Back in school, we dropped our books back in the auditorium and finished our breakfasts.

There was a nervous energy among our group. Excitement mixed with fear.

"We should run the scene one more time," Sam suggested. "Before everyone gets here." Hope and Jason were nodding their heads in agreement, waiting for me to make the decision.

Have to say, I kind of like this directing thing.

"No," I said. "We ran it enough last night. It's good. I don't want us to go second-guessing everything now and screwing it all up. We'll be fine."

I don't think they were entirely convinced, but they didn't push the issue. I was glad, because I was already questioning everything I had told them to do the night before. I didn't want to start changing things over and over again until we were forced to stop. The time for altering the scene was in the past. Now, we just had to trust ourselves. And I had to believe that I hadn't totally screwed my friends' chances.

We went through a few warm-ups together, but took our seats as people started arriving. The Drama Geeks filled the auditorium with a nervous energy as they came in for audition day. Everyone got there early and just about all the groups split off around the auditorium to squeeze the last remnants of rehearsal time out of their scenes.

Not my group. We sat in our seats silently going over our lines and blocking. Keeping ourselves focused and calm. There was no extraneous chatter. No conversation at all. Our unusual behavior drew focus from our classmates, but we ignored them as well. There was no one else in our world but our characters and our scene partners.

Leave it to Holly Mayflower to totally invade without an invitation.

"Giving up already?" she asked as she came into Hall Hall only minutes before we were scheduled to begin.

Sam ignored her.

Hope did not.

"Holly," she said. "I have just now achieved my moment of Zen. Don't make me ruin it by knocking you on your bony ass."

Holly chuckled. "Hope. You are always good for a laugh. But seriously—"

"Holly," I said, interrupting her. (Something I've never done with her before.) "Save it. You're cutting into our prep time. Enough with the stupid games. It's time to let your acting speak for itself."

"Excuse me?"

I gave her a wave of my hand. "You are dismissed."

She laughed in her own dismissive way. "Bryan, it takes a lot of courage to go onstage after what Hart said about you. I just wanted to stop by to wish you all good luck."

Jason gulped in the cool morning air. The guy was freakish about his rituals and Holly had just committed the ultimate sin: Never wish anyone good luck in a theater.

"We don't need luck," Sam said. "We've got talent . . . and a kick-ass scene."

Holly's group left without another word, but Gary did look back to roll his eyes like he knew his scene partner was crazy. We shared a quiet laugh with him and then went back to our sustained silence. Well, after we took a minute to convince Jason that our scene wasn't cursed because of Holly's wishes of luck.

Mr. Randall posted the scene order on the callboard at precisely nine o'clock. Guess he wasn't anticipating any volunteers today. Everyone ran up to see how things were going to play out, but we continued our calm preparations and waited in our seats. Holly's team did the same.

Once the mad rush was over I got up to look. I guess Gary was elected for his group, because he made his way over as well. We arrived at the list together, almost like two gunslingers meeting at high noon. All eyes were on us, like they were expecting a showdown.

According to the order Mr. Randall had laid out, everyone else was going to be our opening acts. He had mercifully chosen my group to go last. Holly's group was the one before ours. I guess we weren't the only ones who thought the decision was going to come down to Sam and Holly.

When Gary and I turned back to the auditorium, we were surprised to see that everyone was still watching us.

"I think they're expecting some macho male posturing," I said to him.

"From us?" he laughed.

I laughed too. We weren't soccer players, after all.

"Break a leg," I said.

"Break two," he replied.

With smiles on our faces, we rejoined our teams and told them when we'd be performing. My group was relieved. Holly looked annoyed. Which only made us feel more relieved.

Mr. Randall got up and said a few things to us before we started. Mostly focusing on how proud he was of all of us for the hard work we'd put in over the program. He tacked on a bit about dealing with criticism at the end and adapting it into a performance. It seemed about a week too late, but it was still appreciated.

Thankfully, he'd also mentioned that Coach Zach wouldn't be bringing the soccer team around this time. A combined sigh of relief washed over the room. It ended abruptly when Hartley Blackstone arrived with his daughter trailing behind him. Mr. Randall barely spoke to our special guest as things got under way. I'm guessing he was a bit peeved at the way Blackstone had thrown the entire program into a tizzy. I threw a smile my teacher's way to let him know his students appreciated the support.

Tasha's group went first. I did not envy them for having to set the tone for the day, but they carried it off pretty well. They'd chosen some obscure scene from a play I'd never heard of, in which Jimmy was supposed to act like a crazy person, tripping over his words and manic in his actions. I wouldn't say he was particularly convincing in his role, but his frantic energy was working for him instead of against him. That way, he wasn't distracting from his teammates' performances.

When they were done, Mr. Randall led us all in a round of applause. This was unusual for scene work. We didn't usually clap at the end. I think he was trying to find a way to combat Blackstone's negativity. I guess we all kind of sensed that, because our applause was more boisterous than the scene deserved.

Blackstone waited for us to die down before he spoke.

"Interesting choices," he said. "Good that you played to the strengths. Thank you."

The stunned expressions of Tasha's group were mirrored in the faces of all the students in the auditorium. As far as we knew, that was possibly the nicest thing the man had ever said in his life. It certainly had to be the briefest. I wondered if this was the same guy who had been there a week earlier.

No dummies, Tasha's group fled the stage before he could say anything else.

The next group consisted of three sophomores doing a scene from, believe it or not, *Miss Julie*. When they were done, our Miss Julie chimed in, along with her father, to compliment them and we all moved on to the next scene.

It quickly became clear that they were just working in anticipation of the final two scenes and the clash between Jason and Gary and, more notably, Sam and Holly. That's not to say that there wasn't some really good scene work being done onstage. Gary's best friend, Madison Wu, was particularly impressive with her Lady Macbeth. But the energy in the room just seemed to be building toward the last scenes of the morning.

It reached a plateau when Holly's group took to the stage.

"I'm Holly Mayflower," she said. "And these are my scene partners, Gary McNulty and Belinda Connors. We will be performing a scene from *A Midsummer Night's Dream*."

What a coincidence. I guess Alexis and Belinda *had* been eavesdropping outside our rehearsal the day we picked our original scene. Holly was going to be so disappointed when she learned that we changed to *Twelfth Night*.

Holly opened the scene with a monologue from early in the play that segued into a scene from the end surprisingly well. She was playing Queen Titania, who had fallen in love with Gary's character while he had the head of an ass (long story). Belinda filled out the scene playing a few random fairies all rolled into a one-role part.

I'd love to say that Holly tanked. That it was a nightmare. But watching her and Gary up there together was really something. As much as I wanted to credit it to Gary's fine acting, I knew it was just as much Holly. Even Belinda was pretty good with the limited material she had.

The applause that came at the end was genuinely enthused. As was Blackstone's commentary. "Quite impressive," he said. "Quite impressive, indeed." He went on to compliment their individual performances in more detail than he had given any other scene critiques earlier. I took this as final confirmation that his choice was going to come from the final two scenes. He even went on at length about the quality of Belinda's performance, which he referred to as "an unexpected gem."

I was so caught up in the excitement of the performance that I almost complimented Holly as we passed when my group took stage. But Holly's smug expression of self-satisfaction stopped any praise that was about to come out of my mouth. I did give Gary a nod of approval. It was clear to me that he was going to be running things once we seniors graduated next year. His smile seemed to double in size when he acknowledged my silent appraisal.

Then. It was our turn.

My group took our positions onstage. As we had agreed, Jason stepped forward to introduce the scene. When he mentioned that Sam was playing the parts of both Viola *and* Sebastian, there was an audible gasp from the audience. I couldn't see Holly's face from where I was standing, but I imagined quite an entertaining reaction there. I wish I could have enjoyed the moment more, but it was time to do our scene.

I was the first to speak. Once I got my two lines out of the way, I stood off to the side and watched the scene unfold. Sam managed her first transition from male to female effortlessly, passing behind one of the two columns we'd left onstage. She came out the other side with an entirely different character just as we'd rehearsed.

Usually, I hated to be in scenes where I didn't have much dialogue. I never knew how to stand there and react in character to what I was hearing from the others. I would always try to project what I was thinking, by nodding in agreement, or scowling, or smiling broadly. In many ways, I was acting with my face, expressing my reactions with no actual feeling behind them. Exactly what Blackstone had been talking about.

This time, I didn't bother listening to the other characters at all. I was watching my friends perform. Any reactions I had were subdued and they were entirely my own. It may not have technically passed for acting, but that wasn't my focus at the moment.

It's kind of crazy watching a scene I'd directed. Jason, Hope, and especially Sam were off and running and I could do nothing to stop them. Not that they needed stopping. Each of them was doing exactly what we had rehearsed—finding their moments and making them their own.

Sam made small adjustments in her movements to differentiate between Viola and Sebastian.

Jason tapped into Orsino's strength to be commanding in his own presence on the stage.

And Hope found the subtleties of a noblewoman, while still bringing her own power to the character.

No matter how good the scene was—and it *was* a good scene—I couldn't stop worrying. About the next line. About the next movement. I was standing in the middle of the scene with absolutely no control over the situation. I had to trust in my actors, to trust in my *friends* to follow the notes I had given them.

And they did.

And it was beautiful.

I didn't need the fierce applause at the end of the scene to know how good it was.

But after the week I'd had, it was certainly nice to hear.

"As wonderfully impressive a performance as the previous one," Blackstone said as the applause died down. "Quite a daring choice to perform both the roles of Sebastian and Viola, Miss Lawson. The way you differentiated between the two characters . . . and the transitions that you made were so . . . so . . ." He snapped his fingers to exemplify his point. It was all we could do not to laugh, considering how we'd practiced those transitions. "Brava."

Sam was beaming. She grabbed my hand and gave it a squeeze of thanks. Personally, that was the only critique I needed, but we weren't finished yet.

"Mr. MacMillan," he said, turning his attention to Jason. "You really brought me into your performance. Opening it up to the entire audience. And Miss Rivera, I was happy to see you break out of your character-part tendencies for a moment somewhere in the middle of the scene."

Sam grabbed hold of Hope's hand before she could react. I suspect it would have been a more visual response than a verbal. With her hand held firmly by Sam, Hope demurely dipped her head in a nod as if she had appreciated his comment. Of course, everyone else in the place knew that her simple move was laced with sarcasm, and got a kick out of it on its own. For a girl known for her bluster, she can do subtle really well.

We all expected him to ignore me like before, but he surprised us all by going, "Mr. Stark you managed to refrain from being a distraction as you stood off to the side. So, that's an improvement."

It was all I could do not to laugh at the pompous—

"What did you think of the staging?" Sam asked before I could finish my thought. She looked at me with a wink. "The direction of the scene?"

Blackstone nodded his head. "There were some nice things in there," he said almost dismissively.

For Blackstone, that was high praise, indeed. He mostly waved it off like it was nothing. And it probably shouldn't have really meant anything to me to hear it, but it did mean something.

It certainly did.

All's Well That Ends Well

We broke for lunch while Blackstone made his decision.
Even though we joked about him going all *American Idol* with
a "You're going to New York! And you're going to New York!"
I could tell Sam was tense. She didn't even try to play with her
food. She merely sat in silence, waiting until it was time to go
back to Hall Hall.

"Hey, it's going to be fine," I said. "That was some of your
most amazing work ever. Seriously. Whether or not you make
it into Blackstone's program, you did your best today. No
doubt." And in my mind, there was none. Sam had a future in
acting, no matter what Blackstone decided. Sure, it would be
easier for her if she got into his program, but aren't people
always talking about how it's the struggle that makes artists
better at what they do? It wasn't like there was a whole lot
of struggling going on at Orion Academy. Drama? Yes. But
actual real-life, hard-core struggle?

Don't make me laugh.

"What was up with that guy being all positive?" Jason asked. "That was a crazy one eighty."

"Maybe he was harsh because he knew we needed to hear it," I said. "He gave us the criticism to help us prepare for the scenes." Okay, I was being all Little Bryan Sunshine, but I was still working off the buzz from our performance.

"And maybe he was back on his meds today," Sam suggested.

We laughed harder than the joke required, but I think we were all enjoying the relief that the most hellacious Summer Theater Program ever was finally over.

Almost.

The entire pavilion went silent when Jimmy ran into the room. Even the soccer team shut up to hear what he had to say.

"He's ready," Jimmy announced.

I don't think the Drama Geeks have ever moved faster in our lives. We were back in Hall Hall in a shot, without a second thought to the food we'd left behind on the tables. Some of the soccer players came along to see what was up. Naturally, Eric and Drew had tagged along. I don't think any of us minded. In fact, I was pretty sure some of us even appreciated it.

Hartley Blackstone was already standing center stage while we filed into our seats. He waited until the room was dead silent before he spoke. "Students of theatre," he said. "I know that this last week was difficult for you. But I think you will all agree that you are now better for it." Well, I doubt that we'd *all* agree, but

I wasn't about to correct him. "That is certainly true for the actor I've chosen for my program. Mr. Jason MacMillan, I look forward to working with you in New York this summer."

The crowd went wild for Jason. Even though we had kind of expected it, the announcement was still exciting to hear. As our group cheered, him on the loudest, Gary leaned over to pat Jason on the back. I was pretty sure that Gary was thinking "next year" to himself while he did it.

Blackstone waited for us to calm down again before he continued. "Now, for the actress, I faced a more difficult decision. Throughout theatre history, leading ladies have often been the most challenging roles to fill. And that was no different here. From the early days of the divine Miss Sarah Bernhardt in Europe, through the evolution of the American Theatre . . ." Oh my God. He was actually going to take us through the history of modern theater before he announced who got the female spot. Clearly, the man loved to hear himself speak. But I'm pretty sure I wasn't the only one who was sick of hearing what he had to say. He continued to ramble on for so long that I almost missed it when he finally announced . . .

"Miss Holly Mayflower."

What?

I couldn't have heard that right. But the choice was confirmed when she actually *stood up to take a bow*.

Sam was all noble, clapping for her rival along with everybody else. Though, I have to admit, the applause in the auditorium was significantly less enthusiastic than it had been for Jason.

Me? I showed solidarity for my sister by sitting on my hands, along with Hope. Childish? Yes. But we were okay with that.

Even Eric was too busy consoling Sam to bother clapping. Again, earning him major points with me. At some point, I was going to have to stop counting and just admit that he was a good guy. Not today, mind you. But at some point.

Once the noise died down again, Blackstone had a few closing remarks before he swept out of the theater. Hopefully, never to be seen again.

Miss Julie then got up and suggested we spend the rest of the afternoon playing more improv games. The sophomores and juniors took her up on it, but we seniors were pretty much burnt by it all. Not to mention that my team was exhausted. It was time for summer vacation to begin. I went home to take a nap.

When I woke, I checked to see if anyone wanted to do that good-bye dinner Sam and I had talked about. Hope already had plans with her dad, which was no surprise. And Sam wanted to spend the evening with Eric so they could give their relationship a name before he left. She was still reluctant about bringing up the whole "exclusive" thing, but I told her that she didn't have to worry. Eric was too good a guy to not want that with her.

I know. I was going soft. But it really was way past time for that.

With nothing better to do, I hopped online to check out the gossip sites for pictures of celebrity dogs. I wanted to focus on helping Mom out more, like Blaine had suggested. Maybe some of her designs would be featured and I could give her an update on what to stock up on.

Color me surprised when I stumbled across an unexpected little entertainment news tidbit. It seems that Mayflower Music was getting into the movie business. And the first film that Anthony Mayflower—Holly's dad—was set to produce was going to be directed by one Hartley Blackstone.

Now, logically, I know that movie deals take forever to put together. And there *is* such a thing as coincidence. But I also know, without a shadow of a doubt, that Holly's father bought her way into the program.

So much for Holly relying on her talent alone. The girl is a Mayflower after all.

I debated calling Sam to tell her what I had found, but what would be the point? Sure, it might reassure her about her acting, but it would also remind her that in our world, no matter how talented she was, there were some ways that she just couldn't compete.

And don't go pitying Sam too much here. My parents can't afford to throw around movie deals for me either.

Since there was no one I could really tell about the Mayflower manipulation, I went back to trolling the gossip sites. On the third site I checked, I found a shot of a three-time celebrity divorcée on the beach with a pair of Welsh corgis wearing outfits from Mom's summer swimwear line. When I called Mom, she didn't even give me a chance to say anything before telling me to meet her and Blaine at our favorite restaurant on Melrose for dinner. She hung up before I could ask what was going on.

I made my way through the traffic and met them an hour later. I'd barely sat when they told me their exciting news. All the extra work they had been taking on lately had been for a very specific reason that had nothing to do with my parents getting divorced or Blaine dying like I had feared. Kaye 9 had grown so popular at the Melrose Avenue location that they could afford to buy a space at Malibu Colony Plaza. Before the end of summer, they would be opening Kaye 9 Malibu right next to the coffeehouse where Sam, Eric, and I had hatched our scheme. It truly was a space worth watching for an exciting new endeavor.

Which meant that I was going to have to start helping out getting the new place ready, bright and early on Monday morning.

My summer vacation was barely going to last one weekend.

But first, Sam and I had to see our friends off Saturday morning. I was in Electra by seven o'clock, picking up Sam and riding out to the Santa Monica Airport. Eric's dad had finagled the corporate jet for a private excursion. Not that it required much finagling since Mr. Whitman owned the corporation. The jet was going to fly Eric and Matthew out to New York, where they would then take a train to the Hamptons to meet up with their mom and her girlfriend. Hope was able to hitch a ride on the jet to spend the summer with her own mom—and Suze—in New York.

It was a morning of so long, farewells, auf Wiedersehens,

and good-byes. Sam couldn't hold back the tears, and I swear I even saw the eyes of her newly exclusive boyfriend, Eric, getting a little moist.

Drew was there too. He and Hope shared a moment saying good-bye for what was likely more than just the summer. In the end, I was pretty sure that those two would always be friends, but maybe a little distance would help with that for now.

We watched the plane take off from the airport's observation deck and stayed until it was a little dot in the sky. With all our friends gone, it looked like it was just going to be Sam and me alone for the summer.

Well, maybe not totally alone. Drew was right there beside me.

And . . . scene.

About the Author

Paul Ruditis started his career as a tour guide at a Hollywood movie studio before working his way up to middle management. One day, he realized that he would much rather be working in his pajamas than in the standard khakis, button-down shirt, and tie. Since that wasn't in line with the studio's dress code, he left to pursue a writing career. He has written and contributed to numerous books based on TV shows like *Charmed* and *Prison Break*. *Everyone's a Critic* is the second book in his original series, DRAMA! It was largely written while the author was wearing pajamas.

★ Show, Don't Tell ★

With only a few days left before the summer curtain falls, Bryan and Sam are looking to end their vacation with a grand finale. It has to be huge. It has to be fab. It has to be . . . medieval?

The Renaissance Faire has come to town! Okay, so the exclamation point doesn't make it any cooler, but Sam is overjoyed to reunite with her former faire folk (say that ten times fast). Bryan, however, can do without the abundance of "thees," "thous," and—oh yes—man tights. But he'd best take part in the festivities lest he lose his head, with Sam doing the chopping.

As if that weren't *dramatic* enough, someone has discovered Bryan's not-so-closeted secret. And although he's never denied it, it might be time for Bryan to step *out* of the role he's been playing for years.

It's a Malibu drama geek stuck with a wannabe King Arthur's dork . . . er, court, and he's got a major secret to tell. You don't want to miss the show. . . .

Public Displays
of
Confession

Like a guilty-pleasure celeb magazine,
these juicy Hollywood stories
will suck you right in. . . .

★ ★ ★

FROM SIMON PULSE ♥ PUBLISHED BY SIMON & SCHUSTER